MW00810681

The Cowboy and His Best Friend

Rock Springs, Texas Book 2

Kaci M. Rose

Five Little Roses

Copyright © 2020, by Kaci M. Rose via Five Little Roses Publishing. All Rights Reserved.

No part of this publication may be reproduced, distributed, or transmitted in any form or by any means, including photocopying, recording, or other electronic or mechanical methods, or by any information storage and retrieval system without the prior written permission of the publisher, except in the case of very brief quotations embodied in critical reviews and certain other noncommercial uses permitted by copyright law.

Publisher's Note: This is a work of fiction. Names, characters, places, and incidents are a product of the author's imagination. Locales and public names are sometimes used for atmospheric purposes. Any resemblance to actual people, living or dead, or to businesses, companies, events, institutions, or locales is completely coincidental.

Book Cover By: **Sarah Kil Creative Studio**

Editing By: Anna @ Indie Hub

Blurb

A best friend's second chance romance. Who meets their soul mate at six years old?

Sage

I met him when I was six. When he saved my life at age ten, we became instant best friends. At age fourteen, I returned the favor. We knew then we had a bond. But who meets their soulmate at age six? Years later, I'm in the hospital again, and he hasn't left my side. Can we put the past behind us? And what about his playboy reputation...

Colt

I knew since I was ten, I would marry her. She would run the ranch with me and be the mother to our kids. Only her. When she ran all those years ago, it broke my heart. After a series of false rumors and misunderstandings, we have another chance now. Only now, I must prove I'm not the playboy this town has made me out to be.

Meet the small town of Rock Springs, Texas with a family that has your back, a town that knows your business, and men who love with everything they have.

There are plenty of horses, nights under the stars, sweet tea, and a few road trips!

Get ready for some HOT Texas Nights!

Warning:

This is a romance with a sexy cowboy and a strong woman who have a lot of heat! This sexy full-length romance. Complete with a happy ever after, no cheating, and no cliffhanger!

This book may have some trigger points centering around abuse and what makes these characters strong and protective and justice is always served!

Readers 18+, please.

Dedication

To the coffee that kept me going and the kids that call me mommy.

Contents

Get Free Books!

Would you like some free cowboy books?
If you join Kaci M. Rose's Newsletter you get books free!
Join Kaci M. Rose's newsletter and get your free books!
Now on to the story!

Read the Audiobook!

This book is also available in audio! Get your copy to listen to as your read.

Get The Cowboy and His Best Friend in Audio

https://www.kacirose.com/BestFriendAudio

Prologue

Sage

Eleven Years Ago

You protect your family.

Always.

That's how Mom and Dad raised me even before they adopted me. Blaze is my best friend and when my bio parents became abusive, he was there for me, and later, so was Colt.

So, when Colt's dad rolls into town, I know I have to be there for him too. Colt's dad is just as abusive as my dad used to be, but Colt's dad only shows up once or twice a year when he needs money. The last time he came in, he wiped out his mom's bank account, stole anything of value from the house, and left all while Colt's mom was at work.

Unfortunately, Colt was home that day and ended up with two black eyes and a broken rib. That was almost two years ago, so we knew he'd be here anytime. We may have only been fourteen, but Colt and I make a vow. This ends this time.

I can only imagine what Blaze would think if he knew. I know he wants us safe, but he has never had to live in that kind of fear. I know what it's like to finally feel safe, loved, and not have to worry. I want to give that gift to Colt.

So, when he doesn't show up to school? I know. I call Mom and make up a story of getting my period and needing to come home to change. I hate lying to Mom, but she picks me up. I think she knows I'm lying. She could have brought me clothes to change into, but she never even suggests it. I just don't think she knows my plans. I know she would stop me.

We live on a huge ranch, so we kids have been driving cars and trucks for a while. Then after everything with my bio parents, I have learned how to shoot a gun, and I'm good. I can hit a moving target spot on. It has made me feel safe knowing I can protect myself even though that scumbag is behind bars for a long time. Maybe my gut knew I'd need it today.

So, when Mom goes to the barn to see Dad, I grab my gun, bullets, and keys to the ranch truck. I leave a note for Mom and head back into town.

Back to Colt, sending up a silent prayer I'm not too late.

On the way, I call Blaze and tell him he needs to meet me at Colt's place. He says he's on the way and for me to wait until he gets there.

It's a ten-block walk from the school.

I have every intention of waiting, I do. But when I get there, I hear screaming and his mom crying. My heart breaks. I whip out my phone, dial 911, and rattle off Colt's address. I leave the phone on the seat, never hanging up, while I jump out and run to his front door before I can think. I see Colt hiding behind the living room couch with his hands over his ears. He's crying. What I see his dad doing to his mom over the dining room table is, well...

I may be young, but I know what rape is. His dad is waving a gun around with a crazy look in his eyes. I know I have to do something fast. The thought of Colt being hurt turns my gut.

I get in the door quietly but not enough. His dad sees me and turns his evil smile on me. He throws his mother to the ground like a rag doll, and she hits her head on the corner of the dining room table. In a split second, I notice the blood coming from the cut. It's a lot of blood.

It's then I see his dad stalking toward me, and I whip out my gun.

Before he can aim his, I pull the trigger on mine. He drops to the floor and red blood pools around his head. I just stand there in shock.

I killed him.

I killed him and I don't even feel bad. What's wrong with me?

I see Colt run to his mom, but I still can't move. My eyes don't leave the blood pooling around his dad's head. The thoughts I have right then surprise me like I wonder how hard it will be to get the blood out of the wood floor.

Then I feel Colt's arms around me, trying to pull me from the house.

"Your mom," I say a bit in shock.

"She's gone, Sage. Let's get out of here."

We get outside and sit on the porch steps. Colt pulls me into his lap and holds me close, running his hands over my arms, asking me over and over if I'm okay.

When I finally look at him, I notice he has a black eye forming and a busted lip. He has a bruise that looks like a handprint on his arm and some blood on his shirt.

Without thinking, I lean in and kiss his black eye ever so gently. His body shudders, and he sighs and pulls me even closer.

"I'm fine. Are you okay?"

He lets out a sigh of relief. "As long as you're okay, so am I."

He holds me and, in his arms, the world doesn't matter. Then I hear him whisper, "Thank you, Sage. I love you, always."

Blaze runs up at the same time the sheriff gets there. Mom and Dad are about fifteen minutes behind them. Colt wants to protect me, but I tell the truth, all of it. The sheriff, a family friend, says it was self-defense, and he will overlook me driving without a license.

I have a hundred hours of community service and several lectures about when to call 911 and doing as the dispatcher says.

Mom and Dad take Colt in, no questions asked. Six months later, he is officially adopted.

A few days after everything settles, Mom and Dad sit with me and ask why I did it. Why I didn't wait for them. They aren't mad. They just want to know.

"You protect family, and Colt is my family."

They tell me they are proud of me but go over all the things I should have done differently. We talk for hours about what I should have done and what happened in detail.

That's why I love Mom and Dad. They may not have liked what happened, but they will share the burden with me.

From that day on, Colt and I share a bond. One that will be tested over and over. In the end, it will be what saves us too. That love is something no one can break.

Not even me.

Chapter 1

Sage

Dammit, how do I always end up in these situations? At least this time, it's just a knife stab. That hurts a lot less than being shot, and the healing time should be less.

At least this time, it wasn't me who killed the bastard.

Two thoughts I never expect to have in my life.

I open my eyes and see Colt standing across the room, looking out the window. The pain in my chest has nothing to do with the slice from the knife and the subsequent stitches.

Earlier today, Jed broke into my house, coming after Riley, my brother Blaze's girlfriend. She had run from him a while ago because he was abusive, and no one in the small town she lived in would help her.

She took off and by the grace of God, a trucker named Lilly picked her up. Lilly brought Riley here in Rock Springs Texas on her regular stop, and somehow Riley ended up in our barn. Blaze hasn't left her side since then. It reminds me of how Colt and I used to be.

When we got her to press charges, Jed fled and later ends up at the house. After some fighting, he sliced my chest deep, but Blaze came in and shot him dead.

Thank God for Texas and the charges already against Jed, the fact he broke in, hit Riley hard, and my knife wound, Blaze won't be charged. The sheriff, who is a family friend, already has promised us that.

My mind thinks back to the last time I was in a hospital bed. Colt was by my side then too. He never left, of course, we were kind of dating then even though no one knew it.

Nine Years Ago

Mac isn't in school today. I know something is wrong. I had seen the signs of abuse. He knows I know, but we don't talk about it. His dad was out of town last weekend for work, so he spent the weekend at home with us.

It's the first time he has been so relaxed, but also the first time I got to see the bruises he keeps covered. Mom and Dad know we have to help him.

But when he doesn't show up at school today, I just know something bad has happened. So, I leave school and go home to get my gun, the one I learned how to shoot better than anyone in town after the issues with my sperm donor.

The gun that freed Colt.

Then I text Blaze and Colt to tell them what's going on. I know they won't be far behind me. Mac lives on the local Indian reservation. But from what I can tell, they have asked too many questions of his dad, so he has been sent to our school in town.

My family has always had a great relationship with the reservation, and I can just hope that keeps up after today.

I get to Mac's house, and I hear the yelling even before I get out of the car. Mac's mom died of cancer a few years back, and his dad hasn't been right ever since. The more he drinks, the worse it gets. Mac has an older sister who is seventeen, and I know he takes the brunt to protect her.

From what I can tell, she turns eighteen in a few weeks and has planned to try to get custody of Mac and get away from their dad. Too bad she can't do it now.

I send a final text to Blaze and Colt telling them his dad is here, and it's bad. They text back, telling me to wait. They are minutes away. I don't answer. I won't lie to them, but I won't wait either.

I get out of the car and peek in a window. I see some movement and notice his sister in the corner crying. She sees me, and her eyes go wide. I hold my finger to my mouth, telling her to be quiet. She nods.

'Where are they?' I mouth. She points toward the kitchen in the back of the house. I can't see them from here, but I can hear them.

I quietly open the door and beckon her outside. She looks toward the kitchen, then moves as quietly as she can.

"Get in my car and lock the doors. Get down on the floor. Take my phone and call 911," I whisper in her ear. She nods and runs off. I quietly move around the room to peek into the kitchen. I see Mac's dad has him pressed against the wall by his throat. Mac, even though he's only thirteen, is an inch bigger than his dad. My heart hurts seeing him like this. Mac has a black eye, a split lip, and a gash at his temple, and he's fighting to stay conscious. I don't have time to wait for Blaze and Colt.

I also don't see his dad has a gun. I step out from behind the wall and say, "Put him down," in hopes of bringing his attention to me. It works, but he pulls a gun on me. Thanks to my training, I pull mine, and we each get off a shot before my world goes dark.

His bullet hits my shoulder, mine hits him between the eyes. I wake up in the hospital room, and Colt is right beside me for the weeks I'm there. He takes me to every physical therapy appointment and is my rock.

A lot has happened over the years, but my feelings for Colt haven't changed. I guess now it's time to face it. After a second near-death experience, I don't have hope to walk out of a third one alive. Now or never.

The rest of my family has been here this evening, but they all have gone home. I know Colt won't leave my side tonight. Blaze won't leave Riley's side, so I know she's safe. Hunter will watch out for Megan, and I know Jason and Mac will watch Mom and Dad. I can relax a bit.

"We need to talk about it," I say.

He turns around, and his eyes snap to mine. I see a split moment of relief seeing me awake and talking before he asks, "About what?"

I take a deep breath. "Why I left."

He paces the room, and I take in his tall six-foot, one-inch build with brown hair and green eyes, a chiseled jaw, a tan from working outside. He has the cowboy body with muscles for days.

He has a new tattoo on his arm that wasn't there when we were kids, but I haven't been able to get a good look at it since we avoid each other as much as possible.

He has always been good looking, even a kid, but it's hard to look at him now and not want to rip his clothes off and have my way with him. I guess that's why I've been avoiding talking to him.

"Not now, Sage," he finally says.

"Colt, it wasn't about you."

"Sure as hell felt like it was."

"I know, it's just..." I whisper but take a deep breath, resting my head back on the pillow. "That night before graduation was the best night of my life."

He looks at me, and his eyes soften. "Mine too," he says and walks back toward the bed.

"But I panicked. Who meets their soulmate at six years old? Then when you said you loved me, you used the same words my sperm donor would say to my bio mom, and I had flashbacks. I freaked out. Okay? I freaked. I was scared, and I didn't know any better."

"Two years, Sage. You were gone for two years."

"I know, but you never called, texted, or came after me either. Then I heard you were sleeping around. I came back for Megan's graduation. I had planned to stay but when Kelli told me you were with her and how she had tamed you and you two were together, I cried myself to sleep that night. I left again the next day." I see his face go pale as I tell him what happened.

"What did she say?"

"Does it really matter?"

"Yes."

I sigh and look up at the ceiling. "She said you were known around town as a great lay and had a new woman every weekend, but she had finally locked you down. She said you two were in love."

He paces again, running his fingers through his hair.

"None of that was true. Dammit," he mutters the last part more to himself.

This catches my attention, and I look over at him again. "What? I still see you two around each other now. What wasn't true?"

"By Megan's graduation, I hadn't slept with anyone. I had been spending time at the bar, but I'd see a woman get trashed. I'd make sure they got home okay. I never touched them, kissed them, nothing."

He pauses and takes a deep breath. "I kept thinking if it was you, I'd want someone to make sure you got home okay. I guess I was hoping if I did enough good, the big man upstairs would watch out for you." Another pause and another deep breath. "When you left after Megan's graduation, I was so mad and hurt. I did sleep with Kelli then. It was only sex, and she knew that from the beginning. It stopped when you came back into town."

I shake my head, trying to make sense of everything. "She was always telling me about all these dates you guys would go on. They always corresponded with nights you came home late."

"So, you believe her over me? After all this time, after everything, what I say means nothing?" He raises his voice.

"No, Colt," I say, barely above a whisper. I can't stop the tears that hit my eyes.

Chapter 2

Colt

Dammit. I don't mean to make her cry. So much has gotten messed up all those years ago, and I feel like we've lost so much time because of lies from people I trusted. Kelli and I are going to have it out at some point, but I need to get Sage to understand.

I've been watching her all day today in the hospital and having flashbacks to when she was in here after everything with Mac. I had known a while ago that I would fight for her but seeing her hurt, it's like a switch flipped. I have failed to do my job and protect her, but I won't fail her again.

She's mine. Mine to protect. Mine to hold. Mine to love. We have a lot to work out, but I'm not backing down. I'm not going anywhere. I don't want to do this here. I want her to rest and heal, but that's my Sage, strong and fierce. When she puts her mind to something, she does it, no backing down.

When I see the tears run down her cheek, everything crumbles. I rush to her side and sit back in the chair, taking her hand in mine. I rest my forehead on them and look at the ground, taking a deep breath. That small contact calms my soul and allows me to think, to breathe.

"I can't take your tears, Sage. I was so scared I lost you today. No matter what has happened, my feelings for you have never changed. It has always been you. It will always be you." I look at her, and I know tears are swimming in my eyes. I will bare my heart and soul to her if it makes her understand my feelings for her.

"I want nothing more than to work through this and have our turn. But not now. Not here. Just let me be here with you and get you back in top shape, so you can kick my ass properly."

She smiles at that and nods. I turn on the TV, and we find a movie to watch, though I'm not watching it. I'm playing over and over in my head the conversation we just had. I'm soaking up the feel of her hand in mine.

I keep playing one sentence over and over in my mind.

Who meets their soulmate at six years old?

We did. The first time I saw Sage, I was hanging out with Blaze. It was the first time I was over at his house, and he wanted to have Sage come over and play with us.

We cut through the trees to the property next door and into the barn. She was in the corner of the hayloft crying. I could see handprints forming on her arm, and her lip was split open, and her cheek was red like someone had slapped her. Because someone had. I knew what happened it is what happens when my father showed up in town.

I dropped to my knees next to her and promised everything would be all right. Her eyes met mine, and I was gone. I didn't know what the feeling was back then. But she had stolen my heart. It was our souls finding each other. I felt it then, she was mine to protect.

I laugh. I've done a shit job at protecting her. She didn't get out of that house for four more years. Then she was shot and now stabbed. I rub my hand over my face.

That day I saw her, Blaze and I got her back to his house and cleaned her up. Not another word was spoken. We spent the whole day with her. The three of us were inseparable after that, not only in school but outside.

I could talk to her about my home life, and she told me hers. When my father wasn't around, my mom was basically a single mom. She worked two jobs. I stayed at Blaze's house a lot, and Sage and I spent many times hiding in the trees between her house and his, just talking.

My favorite times were when we talked about the future. I'd get her to talk about the life she wanted, the home, kids, pets. I wanted to hear it all, so I could make plans and give it to her.

I'm shaken from my thoughts when a nurse enters the room. I see her eyes land on me and watch her back straighten. She pushes her chest out. Great, this is so not what I need after my conversation with Sage.

I watch a pout form on her lips, but she does nothing for me. She has on a bit too much makeup, and you can tell her boobs, while larger, are fake. Pair that with her shift in attitude when she sees me, I know she's all fake.

I look at Sage who is more real than anything. Just looking at her makes my heart race a bit faster. It only does that with her. That's how I know it's always going to be her.

"Visiting hours are over," the nurse purrs with a smile and a pout on her lips, running her eyes up and down my body.

"I'm not leaving. Have security call the sheriff. He will tell you the same thing." After what Sage went through today, everyone knows I won't leave her side. I'm sure the sheriff already cleared it with the staff like he did the last time Sage was in the hospital. I don't know why this girl is even in here.

The nurse twirls her hair, and I know her mind is calculating her next move. I look over at Sage. and she has the same blank look on her face she always does when women flirt with me around her.

Fuck.

I need to prove to her I mean what I say, and I don't want any doubt in her mind. Ever.

This nurse has no idea what she stepped into. She's about to be the first example of the new me. The one who will stop at nothing to get what I want, and what I want is Sage.

"I'm not leaving, and I'm sure your supervisor wouldn't like to hear about you flirting with a patient's visitor when the patient was just in a life or death situation a few hours ago." I hold up my hand that's holding Sage's. "You see this? I'm here for her, not to pick up some floozy nurse."

With that, the nurse gets mad, turns on her heels, and stomps off. Sage stares at me with wide eyes. My face softens instantly.

"What is it, love?"

"You always flirt back and get their phone number," she says. This just proves what an asshole I've been. I have a lot of groveling to do, and if I know Sage, she won't make this easy.

I drop my head and shoot up a quick prayer that I haven't done so much damage that this can't be repaired.

"You're right. I did it to hurt you. You weren't the only immature one, but I threw away every phone number. I never once called any of them."

I look up and meet her eyes. Sage can always tell when I am lying, and I see her studying my face now. Having her gaze on me sends lightning bolts through my body. It's always been electric with us, and knowing that hasn't changed gives me hope.

I watch her move over to the side of the bed and then pat the bed next to her. "Let's get some sleep."

"I can sleep in the chair."

"Colt, I'm pretty sure the bed is more comfortable and after today..." she trails off. "Well, I know Blaze won't come and lie with me anymore now that he has Riley. That leaves you to fend off my nightmares."

That catches my attention. After everything her bio parents did to her, she had nightmares for years, every night, all through school. Hearing her wake up screaming tore my heart out. Eventually, Blaze would lie in bed with her, and the nightmares stopped. Later, when we started high school, Blaze played football, so the nights he couldn't be there for her, I was.

Having an excuse to hold her in my arms all night was something I looked forward to every night. I could have had the worst day but lying with her and pulling her close fixed everything. Waking up with her in my arms always put a smile on my face.

I remember many nights watching her and thinking how lucky I was. I felt complete.

That's what pushed our relationship forward, lying at night with her in my arms. We would stay up and talk or watch TV. Waking up with her in my arms the next morning was like waking up in heaven.

Later, in high school, we chose to sleep in my bed more and more, but nothing would happen. Her nightmares stayed away as long as she wasn't alone. I'm not sure what happened for the two years she was gone but when she came back, the nightmares had stopped.

"You still have them?"

"Only when they're triggered."

Like today. Is what she doesn't say, but we both think it.

I nod, standing. I slip off my shoes and head to the door to close it, leaving just a small crack. I turn off the lights and crawl in bed next to her.

I fall asleep with Sage back in my arms where she's supposed to be.

If I have my way, it's where she will always be.

Chapter 3

Colt

I'm woken up by the morning nurse coming in to do her rounds. Sage is still sound asleep with her head on my shoulder, and I don't move as I watch the nurse.

"I saw nothing." The older lady smiles at me. "You know I was her nurse when she was here last time with the gunshot. You never left her side then either."

"No, ma'am."

She nods looking at me. "You marry her yet?"

I almost swallow my tongue. Never has someone been so blunt about our relationship. Then again, not many people know about us either.

"No, we had some misunderstandings. We're trying to patch them up."

"Well, don't put it off. A love like this is one everyone looks for, but few are lucky enough to find it. Don't let it go."

All I can do is nod while the nurse makes a few notes on her chart.

"And whatever you said to the night nurse, thank you. She's a huge pain in the ass. She's always messing things up that I must clean up. I'm pretty sure the only reason she still has a job is because she's sleeping with the supervisor."

I smile at her. "Yeah, I wasn't exactly nice."

"I wish I could have been here to see it." She gives me a smile and heads back out the door.

•••••••••••

Later that day, the doctor gives Sage the okay to go home but wants her on bed rest until her follow-up appointment next week to get the stitches out. No lifting, no moving her arms above her head, no exercise, and no horseback riding.

I've been texting with Blaze all day. He says Mom and our sister Megan have the house cleaned up, which includes bleaching the blood out of the tile. Blaze has repaired the window Jed broke, so everyone can move back into the house tonight. I guess they all stayed at Mom and Dad's last night.

After Sage's sperm donor went to jail, her egg donor tried to keep the ranch going, but we all knew it was a matter of time before she was forced to sell it, or it went to foreclosure. Sage brought it up to everyone about buying the land when it went up for sale.

We all busted out butts to put money away to buy the ranch. Blaze worked the ranch and was able to sell extra hay, Sage started her horse training, I worked odd jobs in town from cooking in the café to landscaping and even cleaning at the bar. Megan would babysit, Jason worked the bar he now owns and when Mac joined the family after Sage saved him, he started doing odd jobs in town as well adding to the fund.

Even when Sage left, she was picking up jobs and always sending money home. I know mom and dad added any profit from the ranch each year to the fund as well. Two years after Sage left following graduation, the ranch went up for sale, and we had saved up enough for a decent down payment.

As promised, Sage came home then. We bought the land, and her egg donor tried to back out last minute when she found out it was us, but it was too late. We brought in some people from the Native American reservation Mac is from and took some of the money left over from the down payment and had extensive renovations done on the house. It looks nothing like it did when Sage was a kid.

Then Sage shocked us all and said she was moving in and insisted Blaze, Jason, Mac, Megan, and myself move in with her. We all agreed.

It's been amazing living with everyone for the last four years. The house is big enough. We aren't on top of each other, but we always have breakfast and dinner together. Sage insists.

Another text comes in and apparently, Blaze also plans to propose to Riley tonight, and I can't be happier for him. I can tell he's nervous, but I know he picked up a ring a few weeks ago and was waiting for all this stuff with Jed to be over.

We were tossing back and forth some ideas but Sage's was the winner with doing the barn up in twinkle lights and using lights to spell out 'will you marry me' Blaze called Sage 4 times today to make sure she was ok with him marrying Riley.

Sage laughs each time Blaze calls to ask her for permission to propose. Each time, she says she already considers Riley part of the family. During his last call, she tells him she will disown him if he doesn't ask Riley. I get why he's so nervous. There have been many girls in his life that didn't understand his relationship with Sage. They would get jealous, or they would treat Sage horrible behind his back.

We guys all made a pact in high school. We would never marry or even date a girl who didn't truly get along with Sage. Then we made her swear she would tell us the moment a girl was mean to her. Sage said she could take care of herself, and we knew she could. We just didn't want to be with a girl like that. It took some convincing, but Sage agreed.

That night, she had asked me to go for a walk with her. Once we were away from the house, she slammed me up against a tree and said I better not be thinking of dating.

The thought causes me to smile now. I had laughed and wrapped my arms around her. I had said the only girl I wanted to date was her. Then I kissed her hard and flipped us around until she was pressed against the tree. Her jealousy made for one of the hottest makeout sessions we had ever had.

Within an hour or so, Mom picks us up from the hospital, and I sit in the back with Sage and hold her hand. We talk about Blaze's proposal and how nervous he has been. Mom and Sage are laughing about his phone calls today, and it's great to hear the laughter in the truck.

We get Sage home, and I take her upstairs.

"Let's get you settled in bed, and I'll get you some dinner." I take her to my room at the end of the hall. We all agree Sage should get the new master bedroom. This was her family's home. My room is next to hers. Even through it all, I can't stand to be far from her.

Though I love how Sage flipped the house, the wing where all our rooms are now, used to be the guest wing.

"Where are we going?"

"My room, so I can keep an eye on you."

"Colt, take me to my room. You can just stay there. I want my own bed."

"I was looking forward to having you in my bed, love." I pout just a little.

"And I was looking forward to sleeping in my own bed." She raises an eyebrow at me.

I relent. "Anything you want, always."

I do love her room. It's a true master bedroom.

Sage's room is done up in white and creams with light-blue accents. She has a plush carpet on the floor and instead of windows, she has five sets of French doors that she loves opening when the weather allows. She also has dark wood beams on her ceiling, a fireplace with a TV overhead, and a sitting area where often we all end up watching movies at night.

She has a large walk-in closet with a large window in it too. Then there's Sage's bathroom; it's a showstopper. The wood beams on the ceiling continue there, and the bathroom is all white marble and hardwood floors. The walls are a light gray, and the sinks are built into old dressers that are painted white, so there's plenty of storage.

She has a crystal chandelier, and her shower would make anyone drool. It's a walk-in shower done up in river rocks. It has two showerheads and two rainfall showerheads in the ceiling. During Hell Week, when we work sunup to sundown, Sage shares her bathroom with us because those showerheads work magic on your muscles.

Her room has always felt like home to me. I love my room, but when I think of home, I think of hers.

I get Sage to her room and set her up in her bed. Even now, she still takes my breath away. Her tan skin and long, dark-brown hair are a sharp contrast to the white sheets on her bed. She looks like an angel, and I feel so lucky to have her in my life.

We have dinner and start our week-long movie marathon. Sage takes pity on me and picks out an action film, but I know there will be plenty of chick flick too.

I will watch every one of them too because I'm not leaving her side.

Chapter 4

Sage

I won't lie, waking up this morning in Colt's arms has been amazing. He hasn't left my side unless it's to use the bathroom or get me food, or anything else I ask for. He has been my sweet Colt from all those years ago.

The Colt only I get to see. That thought does funny things to my heart.

He's different though too. Instead of the unsure boy who was learning as we went along, he has a hot alpha-male vibe to him now. He knows what he wants, and he's going after it. Instead of the thin growing boy that was all knees and elbows, he's now all man with muscles for days and tattoos I just want to run my tongue over.

We've both grown, and I'm excited to learn more about my best friend and the Colt only I get to see. He's downstairs now refilling our snacks and waters, and I'm so lost in thought I don't hear Riley come in until she jumps on the bed beside me, laughing.

I know Blaze proposed last night, and I know she said yes. I just wait for her to talk.

"Sage! I'm getting married!" she squeals, and I laugh. I'm so excited for her. She isn't like the other girls the guy's have dated. Many of them were sweet as sin to them and turn on me the second their backs were turned.

No, Riley is the whole package and so good for Blaze, and she's quickly becoming one of my best girlfriends.

"Tell me everything."

I listen as she tells me about Blaze's proposal and how they stayed up late talking and making plans.

"Please tell me you guys will stay in the house with us at least until you have kids. You can slowly remodel one of the houses on the ranch for later," I beg her.

"Oh, of course, we're going to stay! I love it here! Oh, Sage. Thank you again, not just for the other day but for everything. For helping me and giving me this family I never thought I would get to have."

"Riley, you were meant to be here, and I love you so damn much."

"I love you too, Sage," she says with tears in her eyes and hugs me so gently. "Would you be my maid of honor?"

"Riley, of course! But you better clear that with Blaze. We always said I would stand with him on his wedding day."

She laughs. "I think he will give into anything I want."

"I think you're right. So, you thinking of a wedding at the church at the other end of the ranch?"

"Actually, I was hoping you would let us get married in the barn."

"The event barn?"

"No, the one out here. It's where we met, where he proposed. I feel like it's where our story began and where this chapter in our life should continue."

I can't stop the smile that spreads on my face. "There have been so many bad memories there. I think we're overdue for some good ones! What about the reception?"

"That we can do at the event barn."

"Love it! Timeframe?"

"Blaze wants to get married this weekend. I said a year, and he growled and said two weeks. I said nine months, he said one month. So, we still haven't settled on a timeframe. I agreed to go dress hunting first and then make plans from there. The dress is the one thing I won't compromise on, and he agreed.

I can't help but laugh at that. "It seems the men in this family, when they meet their soulmates, are impatient and go all Alpha on us."

She laughs then looks at me. "So, Colt?"

"He hasn't left my side other than to get me food."

The thought makes me smile. He's still my Colt, the one that always makes sure I'm okay. For that reason alone, I know I will try with all this but to be honest, I don't know if we can move past everything.

We have both hurt each other so much over the years. Can we heal from that?

"Have you talked?"

"Actually, yes. We talked last night after everyone left." I go on to tell her about the conversation and the misunderstandings, the event with the nurse, and how he's staying here with me in my room.

When I'm done, her jaw drops. "Wow, so what are you going to do?"

I sigh. "I don't know. I want to talk this out, but I'd be lying if I didn't say I was scared. We hurt each other so much, I'm scared we can't heal from it. There have been so many misunderstandings, I'm worried we'll only be reopening old wounds."

"Oh, you will be, I'm sure of it."

I roll my eyes. "Thanks for the pep talk."

She laughs. "But it has to happen for you two to move on. You need to heal right and to do that, you have to reopen the wound and set it right."

I sigh. "When did you become so smart?"

"When I started hanging around you."

I laugh. She stays, and we hang out and talk for another hour about wedding plans and school she's getting ready to start.

Soon as she leaves, Colt is right there, ready to crawl back into bed with me.

"You don't have to stay with me, you know. I'm sure there's plenty more you need to be doing."

"I'm right where I need to be, here with you."

"You have to be bored to death."

"I have you in my arms. Everything is perfect."

I roll my eyes.

"What? You don't believe me?"

"I'm bored already one day in, how are you not?"

He smiles. "It's been so long since I've gotten to hold you like this, Sage. I'm enjoying every minute of it. I don't care if we watch *The Notebook* on repeat for a week, I'll never get bored of having you in my arms."

Damn, he makes my eyes water. Just to prove his point, he puts on *The Notebook*, and we settle in to watch TV, eat snacks, and talk about Blaze's wedding plans and the ranch.

During an action movie we watch later, one I picked just for Colt, I close my eyes and fall asleep with a smile on my face.

Chapter 5

Colt

Waking up again this morning with Sage in my arms is something I will never get tired of. I don't know how I'm going to sleep in my bed alone ever again. I look over at Sage. God, she's the most beautiful woman I've ever seen. Even as kids she was the most beautiful girl.

She has it all. She's breathtakingly beautiful but doesn't know it. She's sweet and caring. She lights up a room with laughter, no matter where she is, and she's strong as hell. It just reaffirms what I've always known. It will always be her for me. No one else, and I won't pretend otherwise.

She's still sleeping facing me. I carefully roll to my side and take her in. Her dark-brown hair and eyes that I know are the most stunning hazel color. They sparkle green when she's happy, turn blue when she's turned on, and go dark brown when she's mad. Eyes that I still see every time I close mine.

I lightly brush a piece of hair from her forehead, and her eyes flutter open. Her eyes lock with mine, and neither of us says a word or moves. The whole room falls away, and it's just me and her. I lightly run a finger over her temple, down her cheek, and across her jaw.

Breathing picks up, and her nipples get hard under her thin t-shirt. I'm glad I'm not the only one that still gets turned on by the slightest touches. It's always been this way between us. I'm rock hard just being able to touch her like this.

I have to remind my cock to stand down. This isn't about us, it's about what she needs. Right now, she needs is to heal and trust us again. We both need to heal and talk. I want a real relationship, not just sex. He doesn't seem to care though.

"Let me take you to dinner when you get the okay from the doctor."

"Colt..." she whispers.

"Please. I want to give us a real chance to work everything out. That's all I'm asking for and if we just end up friends, so be it."

Lie.

We won't end up just being friends. I'll never be okay with just being friends again.

"But I want to work this out. I want to work through this and put it all behind us. During that time, I don't want you seeing anyone else, and I won't either. I just want a chance."

"Colt, I don't know..."

"I want to take you out, show you off, and let the whole town know it's always going to be you. So, everyone leaves me alone. This is it for me. No more games. One month. Give me one month," I plead.

I see her looking into my eyes, and I try to convey everything I can't put into words. I don't know what she sees, but it works.

She takes a deep breath and nods. "One month."

I can't stop the smile that spreads across my face if I tired.

Sage

It's been a week since I agreed to give Colt one month. My stitches are out, and I'm allowed to move around but not to lift anything heavier than my purse, so I've taken over all the bookwork for the ranch, so I don't feel quite so useless.

I love being out on the land, getting dirty, being with the animals. Paperwork has always been part of running the ranch, but I hate spreadsheets and accounting. But it has to get done so the ranch hands get paid.

I told Mac when he earns his degree, I'm secretly hoping he'll take up accounting and do all the bookwork for us, but he's like me. He loves getting dirty and being with the animals. So, Blaze and I take care of the bookwork with help from Colt and Dad.

Tonight is my first official date with Colt. We dated in high school, but it just progressed that way. There was never an official date especially since we weren't telling people about us. We spent a lot of time together, and I could pick many moments I'd consider a date, but I'm not sure what our first date really was.

It might have been the picnic after our first kiss? Maybe? Either way, I will remember this night, so I'm going all out!

I decide on a lace, off the shoulder dress in a vintage peachy coral color. The sleeves are long and flowy, but the neckline is high enough to cover where the knife sliced me, which is healing nicely. The dress is on the shorter side, kind of like an oversized shirt that hugs all the right places and still covers everything.

I pair it with my ivory lace and glitter cowgirl boots and a silver and turquoise necklace Colt bought me at the reservation our senior year of high school. I haven't been able to bring myself to wear it again but now seems like the perfect time.

I head downstairs to meet Colt and when his eyes meet mine, his jaw drops. I can't help but smile. I nailed the outfit; the fact I can cause a guy to have that reaction is a huge confidence booster. But Colt having that reaction? It sends the butterfly in my stomach on overdrive.

"Wow! You look stunning, Sage." He takes my hand and leans in to kiss me on the cheek. He leads me to his truck and helps me in, making sure I'm buckled in before rounding the truck and getting in himself.

We drive in silence until we get to the end of the dirt road. He stops and looks at me.

"Listen, thank you for doing this tonight. I want to show you off because, wow, that outfit needs to be shown off. I want everyone to know that no matter how this ends, I'm yours.

I want to have dinner and enjoy ourselves. I want you to tell me about your travels and everything I missed. Then I was thinking we could head out to our old spot by the church and talk some?"

I sigh. That's my Colt, always with a plan. "Okay." I smile and relax.

"Once we put this all behind us, if this doesn't work out, if we can't move past this, I want nothing more than for you to be happy... even if it isn't with me."

I look at him. I see my unsure boy who is scared to make the wrong move, scared to lose me. A stab of guilt hits me. He lost me anyway, and it was nothing he did. But there's a part of me who is sick at the thought of this not working out.

Would he date again? Would he go back to Kelli? Could I stand to see him with anyone else? I sure as hell can't stand the thought of him with Kelli. No way in hell will I allow her on my land...

Almost like he can sense me going down that road, he pulls me back to him. "It would crush me. I won't lie, but I need you to be happy."

If I were standing, I'm pretty sure I'd be swooning right now. It breaks my heart and makes me fall for this man even more if that's possible. I steel my nerves and make myself a promise that I will make sure we can come on the other side together.

I reach over and take his hand in mine, intertwining our fingers all the way to Jason's bar. It's called WJs, but everyone calls it Waylon's after its original owner. He left the bar to Jason when he died since none of his kids wanted it.

The bar has changed, and Jason is now adding food to the menu. Everyone likes it as long as he keeps the bar, stage, and dance floor.

This is the perfect place for our first date, near family with food, music, and dancing. I look over and smile at Colt whose smile matches my own.

Chapter 6

Sage

My nerves hit as we walk through the door, but he, as always, is there with his hand on my lower back, using his thumb to rub circles and easing my nerves without a word.

We sit toward the back, and I take in the place, it hasn't changed much. When you walk in, there are tables in front of you, but you have a clear shot of the stage and the dance floor. To the right, towards the back, is the bar. This is Jason's baby.

He has upgraded this area quite a bit, doing most of the work himself. He's won a few competitions around the state, and the awards are displayed on the top of the open wood cabinets along the back wall. Mounted on the back wall, he has made an American flag out of beer and soda cans. The liquor and glasses are all displayed in the open wood cabinets around the flag.

The whole bar has wood paneling from old barns around the area. Each section has the barn's info and the family it belonged to. Lots of Texas and ranching related décor hang along the walls.

Each local ranch in the town has its brand on the wall around the bar. Since this is a family bar, and we're the second biggest ranch in the state and the largest in this area, ours is proudly displayed near the bar. I think Jason likes having it close. It's a sign of what we all worked our butts off for.

We get a few of the new dishes Jason wants us to try out. Jo, the café owner, wants to close for dinner. Breakfast is her biggest moneymaker, and she's open for lunch. Since Jason plans to open for dinners soon, she'll close later in the afternoon. I guess she plans to offer the café as an event space to make up for any money lost there. More money, less time. I don't blame her.

Colt and I talk about my travels for the two years I was gone. I tell him about watching the sunrise on Cadillac Mountain in Acadia National Park in Maine, swimming with dolphins in Florida, driving Route 66, and touring Alcatraz.

"Is there anything you didn't get to do that you wanted to?" his eyes watch mine.

"Alaska and Hawaii. I want to see Pearl Harbor, hike a volcano, see the Northern Lights and climb a glacier. I want to hike Angel's Landing in Zion National Park, but if I'm honest, I'm too scared to do it alone."

"Any plans to leave again and finish the list?"

I reach out and grab his hand and smile. "Someday. I was thinking I'd skip out on one of the weeks at the lake house with the family and go to Hawaii next. I was going to ask Blaze to go with me, but I doubt that's an option now."

"I'll go with you. Just say when."

I can't help the smile that spreads across my face. Traveling with Colt is at the top of my bucket list. The one thing I have been scared to ask for.

"What finally brought you home?"

"I was at the Grand Canyon with Blaze when Dad got the call that my family's land was going up for sale. I always promised I'd come home if it did. We had all worked so hard for it, so I kept my promise. If I didn't know any better, I think Blaze and Dad timed it. Blaze had been bugging me since he got there about coming home."

We dig into our food, and Colt tells me how he's been doing work at the reservation and helping them with some of the ranches there.

After dinner, he asks me to dance. The last time I danced with anyone was with him at prom. I know I'm a little rusty.

We dance a few quick two steps before the music turns slow, and he pulls me in. We sway to the music. I notice I'm getting more than a few dirty looks from the girls in the room.

Colt must feel me go stiff because his hot breath is on my ear. "Ignore them. Jason has our back. I already talked to him. Plus, this is what I want. I want them to know it's always been you, and it will always be you."

I stay silent just looking into his eyes.

"They're mad because I always refused to dance with anyone. The last person I danced with was you at prom."

Little by little, he heals my broken heart, and he doesn't even know it. Knowing I'm the only person who has ever and will ever have a part of him like this, no matter how small, it's something big to me.

"Really?" I can't help but ask.

"Yes. I know I messed things up but only you have had my heart. Only you have gotten dates, and only you have gotten the romantic part of me." He brings his hand up to the side of my face, and his thumb rubs my cheekbone.

"I will say it until the day I die. It has only ever been you, and it will only ever be you." His eyes travel down to my lips, and I watch the heat flare in his eyes. My tongue darts out and wets my lips, and his eyes snap back to mine.

I can see a split-second decision being made in his eyes before he leans in, pausing just enough to let me pull away if I wanted to. Newsflash, there's no way in hell I'm pulling away from this kiss. A second later, his lips are on mine, right there on the dance floor in front of everyone.

This is the first time since graduation night that our lips have touched. That was seven years ago. But right now, at this moment, it feels like no time has passed. This kiss is soul searing and melding our souls back together. I feel it.

His other hand moves to my face, and he takes control of the kiss. Holy hell, Colt is an amazing kisser. It's a hard but sweet kiss, possessive but caring. It steals my breath away. One hand moves to the nape of my neck to pull me in closer.

This tender yet possessive kiss has my panties soaked and me forgetting where we are. All I can see, hear and feel is him. The bubble around us bursts a moment later when a few whistles from around the bar catch our attention.

Colt pulls away but stops me from looking around the bar again.

“Don’t look around. Keep your eyes on me. Don’t let them ruin this. That was the best damn kiss of my life, Sage. Better than all of our kisses before this.”

My eyes meet his, and he has the look on his face that I have dubbed as my look. All these years later, I now know that look is a look of love and passion. But it’s still my look, and this is the first time I’ve seen it in seven years.

“Mine too,” I whisper, and it causes him to close his eyes. He takes in a deep breath that makes his body shutter.

“Keep dancing with me?” I ask, not wanting to let him go just yet.

“Anything you want, love.” We dance through several more songs before we head out.

In true Colt style, he walks me to his truck, opens his door, helps me inside, and waits until I am buckled in before closing the door and heading around to get in. I turn sideways in my seat to watch him as we drive out to the church at the edge of the ranch property.

When Dad's ancestors settled here, there wasn't a church, so they built one. It's small but beautiful and while it hasn't held weekly service in over forty years, it is still used for family weddings and funerals.

As we pull out of the parking lot, Colt looks over at me watching him, and reaches out to take my hand.

"I've had a really good time tonight, and no matter how the conversation goes tonight, I want to go out again," I say.

"Yeah?"

I smile. "Yes."

"Deal." He squeezes my hand. For the rest of the drive, we talk about the bar and the changes Jason is looking to make.

Before I know it, we park in front of the old church. Colt turns off his headlights and rolls the windows down before turning the truck off. We both remove our seatbelts and turn to face each other.

"Remember the night after I was adopted, we snuck out here after dinner?" he reminds me.

“When we sat in the back pew and talked about being a real family.”

“Yeah, we talked for hours, and I don’t remember what we talked about. I remember just wanting to hear your voice and be with you,” he says. “I knew then I was in love with you. I just didn’t understand it all, ya know?”

I nod because I know exactly what he means. We’re both quiet, looking at the church. Lots of good memories here. We loved to sneak out here and just talk. Later, we had quite a few good makeout sessions there too. It was also one of our spots we would meet when we needed to talk.

I can tell by the look on his face, he’s remembering those memories as well. Almost all of them are good. Many of those memories I have pulled out to get me through the hard times over the last few years.

Looking in the backseat, I see a few pillows and blankets and smile.

“Want to make up the bed in the back like old times?”

He smiles. “I was hoping you would want to.”

Chapter 7

Colt

One of our favorite dates used to be parking my truck out somewhere on the ranch and making up the bed of the truck with pillows and blankets and just lying down, taking it all in, and talking.

Many times, it's lying under the stars, but we have seen many sunrises and sunsets as well. We also had our first hot and heavy makeout session down the creek under the stars. Then later, we made love several times under the stars as well. While I don't plan to get that lucky tonight, those memories aren't far from my mind, and my cock is making it well known.

I grab the pillows and blankets and set up the bed of the truck. Then I help her climb on in. We get comfortable and stare up at the stars in silence for a bit.

I know what we need to talk about, but I just don't know where to start. I'm not in a rush to dampen the mood on what has been one of the most perfect nights I've had in years.

She speaks first, and I listen to every word.

"That first year I traveled, I didn't go on a single date. Many guys asked. They asked to take me to dinner, or for a dance. Some were bolder and asked to go back to their place. I said no every time. Never crossed my mind to answer them any other way. I was yours and to me, that hadn't changed. Some of those guys turned into friends, and we have kept in contact, but they know they're permanently friend zoned."

I reach over and take her hand, needing some connection with her. I don't know what the conversation ahead holds, but I know it will be easier with this small connection. She interlaces our fingers and keeps talking.

"But after Megan's graduation... when I left, I went out with the first guy who asked. We dated for a few weeks and one night, things got to third base. I did what I do best and panicked. I packed up and left that night I texted him the next day that we were over and moved on."

She pauses and looks up at the sky like she's trying to choose her words, so I squeeze her hand to encourage her. I'm torn on if I want to hear this story, but I also know we must get it out in the open to move on.

"After that, I went on a few dates, but it never went that far again. Then I talked to Blaze. We were making plans for our Grand Canyon trip, and he told me about you and Kelli, and I broke. I went to a local bar, had a few drinks, and had my first-ever one-night stand. I don't know if you even want to hear this, but the whole time, I was thinking of you. I got home that night and cried myself to sleep."

My heart breaks. I never wanted to cause her that kind of pain, but so many times I was so hurt that I did want to hurt her. The thoughts of her crying herself to sleep I can't take, even if I wanted to pound my chest that it was me she thought of when she was with another guy.

We're both quiet, soaking that news in. I reach over and pull her towards me. We still don't look at each other, but she rests her head on my shoulder. I run my hand up and down her back.

"Were you with anyone before Megan's graduation?" she asks.

"No, I wasn't." The thought of that kills me. If Kelli hadn't interfered, we could have fixed things then. We would have, I know it. The thought angers me. I still need to have it out with Kelli. I don't like her thinking she won this, even though I know Sage will say to let it be.

"Kelli and I did sleep together after Megan's graduation on and off, but we stopped when you came back to town. Then she and I slept together once when you were dating that guy from Dallas and when you dated that rodeo guy. That was the last time. I made the choice awhile back that I would try to fix this with us, so I cut her off completely. I never knew how to go about things with you. Then Riley showed up, and I put it on the back burner again. But when I saw you with Brice..."

She cuts me off then. "It wasn't serious with Brice. I was just so sick of being lonely and even more so watching Riley and Blaze fall in love. I didn't want to go to the sale alone, so I went with Brice."

She squeezes my hand then tries to lighten the mood. "He was a horrible kisser."

I can't help but smile. "Good." But then I have to know. "Did you... with him..."

"No, Colt. We kissed a few times, and that was it. It never went any further."

I feel myself relax at that.

"Has there been anyone other than Kelli?"

"I had two one-night stands in Dallas years ago, but for the record, Sage, I haven't been with anyone in almost two years now."

I can tell she's smiling when she says, "Good."

"Has there been anyone since your one-night stand?" I ask. I have to know, but at the same time, I don't want to know. Not that it makes a difference. There could have been a hundred guys, she'd still be mine.

"No. I thought about it, but I just didn't have it in me. It's been over five years since I've been with anyone," she says, in a whisper.

I nod, and my heart swells. So many misunderstandings were just cleared up tonight. I don't think it was as bad as either of us thought.

Almost like she can read my mind, she says, "Can we put this conversation on pause? I'd like to end tonight on a good note."

I agree. Having good memories of our first date after all this time is all I want for her.

After a minute, she rolls over to her side so her chest is pressed to my side. Her head is on my shoulder, and her hand is on my chest. I wrap my arm around her back and place my hand on her waist. With my free hand, I hold hers. When I take a deep breath, it's shaky. Does this girl know what she does to me? Is it too much to hope I have the same effect on her?

"This okay?" she asks. How can she not think this is okay? I need to make sure she knows I'm here waiting like a stray dog, to soak up any attention she wants to throw my way. Some might say that's sad and pathetic, but when you meet Sage and you know what it feels like to have her attention, you would understand.

"More than okay," I say and kiss the top of her head. "I missed this."

"Me too," she whispers then looks up at me. When she smiles at me, my heart takes off like a racehorse at the Kentucky Derby. I lean into her, rolling her gently onto her back, and kiss her.

Without breaking the kiss, I roll on top of her and brace my weight on my arms by her head. She sighs, and I take the opportunity to explore her mouth. When her tongue meets mine, I'm as hard as steel, and I know in this position, she has to feel me. I want her to feel me, to know the effect she has on me.

She wraps her arms around my neck and pulls me even closer to her. I kiss down her neck and stop at the spot where it meets her shoulder, causing her to moan. As I kiss back up to her jaw, I watch her every move and see if the same spot on her neck just under her ear drives her crazy still. While I lightly scrape my teeth over it, she moans my name, and I can't help but smile.

I kiss my way back to her mouth again, and we make out like teenagers for a long while, neither of us pushing to take it any further. I'm going to have a major case of blue balls that no cold shower will help, but it's worth it with her.

When I finally pull away, I rest my forehead on hers to catch our breath.

"Can I take you out tomorrow night?" I ask her.

"Well, I have to be up early on Sunday morning."

"For church, right?"

She gives me this strange look, but she will soon know that I know everything about her. Every move she makes, what she likes and hates. I never stopped watching and paying attention.

"Yes, how did you know?"

"I pay attention." I pause. "Can I come with you to church?"

With this, she sits up with her back to the window of my truck. I sit up facing her with her hand in mine.

"You want to go to church with me?" she asks in shock.

I smile. "Yes, and the potluck after. I know you and Mom go every week."

I can tell she's thinking about it and running it over in her head.

"Okay then, what about a running into town date tomorrow. I need to pick up feed and a few things. We can do lunch at the café?"

I smile. "Perfect."

We head home, and I walk her to her room and give her a chaste kiss.

"See you tomorrow, love," I say then head to my room. Even though I have spent a week in bed with her while she was healing, I don't want her to think this is about sex.

Sleeping in my room with her just next door is the hardest thing I've ever had to do after the night we just had.

Chapter 8

Sage

I slept worth a crap last night. I got so used to Colt sleeping next to me, it was almost impossible to sleep last night. I kept thinking of going into Colt's room. I know he wouldn't have turned me away, but I just never got up the guts to do it. It was well after three a.m. before I finally got to sleep.

We're now riding into town and even though we're taking my truck, Colt insists on driving. We fight a bit but when he says it's a small way he can take care of me, I swoon a bit and give in. I haven't let go of his hand since we've been in the car though.

We make a few stops before filling up the back of the truck at the feed store and then head to the café next door for lunch. Jo is working, and her whole face lights up when she sees us. She comes over and gives us both a hug.

"I heard you two made quite a show last night at the bar. I am so happy for you two. I always loved seeing you two together! Come. Sit at the table back here, less prying eyes," Jo says.

Colt sits next to be me instead of in the booth across from me.

I look at him, and he can see the question in my eyes right away.

"The other side is too far away." He pouts, and it's so cute, I can't help but laugh. Then I see everyone in the café is watching us. Some are being blatantly obvious, and some are trying to make it look like they aren't, but they are. I see some are texting on their phones, so I know the word is spreading that we're here.

"Ignore them all. It's just you and me, Sage." He leans over and kisses my temple. We both look over the menu though it hasn't changed in years. Jo's motto is if it ain't broke, don't fix it.

Jo comes over to take our order. "We will both have the meatloaf. Extra gravy on hers and an order of cornbread. Sweet tea for both of us," Colt orders for me.

I can't help but stare at him as Jo walks away. He seems to be staring then shifts in his seat a bit.

"What? Did I get it wrong?" he asks.

I don't answer. I just lean in and kiss him. It's a short, sweet kiss. "I forgot what it's like to be with someone who knows me so well. The order was perfect."

He beams then leans in for another quick kiss. People file in to get takeout orders or even just to-go coffees, and every one of them looks over at us. I now understand what zoo animals feel like.

We have a few people come up to tell us it was about damn time we got together which makes us laugh. We talk about food, the ranch, hobbies, and just get to know each other again.

We're about halfway through our meal when someone sits in the booth across from us. I look up and see the bottle-blond hair of no other than Kelli. She doesn't look like she's here to congratulate us. Colt's hand on my thigh tightens, and I feel his whole body go stiff.

I look at Kelli for the first time in a while. She looks a bit like a blond Lindsay Lohan before the drugs, but she just looks fake. Fake hair, fake nails, fake boobs, fake eyelashes, caked-on makeup. Then it hits me. She's the exact opposite of me, and it makes me laugh.

Out loud. Earning me a glare from fake Barbie.

"What the hell, Colt?" she whines, and her voice is like nails on a chalkboard. High pitched and whiney, and I now hate my spot trapped in the booth.

"Go away, Kelli. There was never anything between us, and the lies you told Sage show how pathetic you are."

I see Kelli's eyes go stormy. "I don't know what you mean, but I never talked with Sage..."

"Cut the bullshit, Kelli. It was just sex. My heart has always been Sage's and because of your lies and scheming, you pushed us away when we could have patched things up years ago. Even if Sage never forgives me, I never want another thing to do with you."

"You will see what you're missing, Colt. I just hope I'm here when you open your eyes."

Colt looks right at me and without breaking eye contact with me, he says, "I already found what I was missing, and she's the nicest, sweetest person I've ever met. She's the exact opposite of you. I've missed her like crazy, and she has always owned my heart and soul. I have no intention of letting her go again." Then he leans in and kisses me.

Kelli lets out some annoying screech that reminds me of a bobcat. That's when Brice shows up next to our table.

"Kelli, it's time for you to go," he says.

"Go away. This doesn't concern you," she snaps.

"No, it concerns the whole café now. You're making an ass of yourself, and Jo just called the sheriff. I think you should leave of your own free will."

She shoots me a death glare then stands, her back ramrod straight. I want to take some dig at her, but how can I top Colt's reply?

Kelli pushes past Brice and walks out of the café. The whole crowd erupts in cheers as she walks out the door, causing her to spin on her heels and stare at everyone before she leaves.

"Thank you, Brice," Colt says and shakes his hand.

He smiles. "Treat her good, or I'll be joining the line of people kicking your ass," he says to Colt.

Colt nods and a look of understanding crosses between them before Brice heads back to his table.

"Eat up, love. Don't let this ruin our day," he says and kisses my temple. No matter how hard we try, we can't get the conversation to flow as easily as before.

As we head out of the café, Colt pulls me the opposite way of the parking lot. "Let's take a walk down Main Street. The weather is nice, let's enjoy it," Colt suggests, and I agree.

We walk down Main Street hand in hand, checking out some shops and antique stores. It feels great to not have to hide like we did in high school. We never got the chance to be open about us, to be able to walk down the street hand in hand like we can now.

Somehow, my gut tells me we haven't seen the last of Kelli, but I push it aside and just try to enjoy the day.

The easy conversation returns when we get back in the truck and head for home. It wouldn't be a Rock Springs date without drama, so all in all, it is still a great day.

Chapter 9

Sage

With yesterday's drama at the café forgotten, we're now sitting in our pew at church. Mom and Dad are to my right and Colt is to my left at the end of the pew. I make a joke that it's the best place for him to make a quick exit. He doesn't find it funny. Once again, all eyes are on us. I think more so today than yesterday.

When Pastor Greg takes his stand at the pulpit and scans the crowd like he always does, I know he takes count of who is here and who isn't. When he sees Colt, his eyes go wide, and he starts the service like nothing is out of the normal.

As we stand and sing, Colt wraps his arm around my waist and shares my hymn book. We're in a small Southern town, and this small action still means something. It means we're a serious couple. I know this is Colt's way of once again staking his claim to me.

Mom and Dad haven't stopped smiling since they saw Colt walk in with me. I did give Mom and Dad a warning he was coming last night which led to a lot of questions, but they did give us their blessing. I guess Colt talked to them too once he told me he was coming.

Being their opinion was one of the things that scared us last time, this is a weight off my shoulders. Though I know if we were still in high school, things would be different. We were still kids, still living under their roof then.

The next battle is talking to Megan, Mac, and Blaze. Jason already knows because Colt talked to him before our date at the bar, though I don't think he knows the details. Riley knows because she picked up on how we act around each other weeks ago. I have given her just enough info, but she doesn't know the details either.

If I'm being honest, I'm terrified to tell Blaze. Not to beat around the bush but keeping this from him is like flat-out lying to him. He's going to be hurt and mad, and I can't blame him one bit. I just hope that since

Riley is on our side, she will help rein him in and talk to him.

After the service, we head to the event room for the church potluck brunch. Colt gets a few dirty looks as we make our way into the room, but most everyone, including Pastor Greg, is welcoming of him. Mom and Dad stick near us almost like we're going to battle.

We pretty much are. We're making a statement that not only are Colt and I together but that Mom and Dad approve. Colt's reputation will factor into the gossip.

We make our way over to fix our plates of food.

"What's good?" Colt asks.

"I brought the taco salad. Mom brings her biscuits and some jam, Miss Dorothy makes the pizza rolls, and everything else is pretty good." Then I think again. "Avoid the Jello... just trust me."

We sit at a table with Mom and Dad. People come over to talk a bit while we eat. When we're done, we mingle a bit more, and that's when Miss Dorthey Carrey herself comes over. Dorthey is a leader of the church's widow club, also known as the best gossips in town. I'm sure they elected Dorothy to come over and get the juicy details.

"Well, Heavens to Betsy, how did you manage to drag Colt here today, Sage?" she asks me.

Yup, she's the one who was nominated to speak for the group. I see her group of friends whispering and watching our every move.

Before I can even come up with a response, I feel Colt place his hand on my waist.

"I told her I wanted to come. She's giving me a chance, and I know the church is important to her, so that makes it important to me."

Then Dorothy looks right at me like Colt isn't even standing right next to me and whispers loudly enough for him to still hear, "You do know about his reputation, right?"

I instantly straighten my back. It looks like we're going to battle right here and now.

Colt starts to say something, but I place my hand on his chest and say, "I know this town likes to gossip, but you have to go straight to the source. That's what I did. As much as I love this town, I'm ashamed of how the gossips turned the good deeds into something horrible and twisted."

I hadn't realized I had raised my voice until I see Dorothy's jaw drop, and the room goes quiet. I'm proud to say I keep my voice steady even when I feel anything but.

Colt leans over to whisper in my ear, "Love, it's okay. We don't have to explain ourselves to anyone. You want to get out of here and get some ice cream?"

I take a deep breath and nod. Just like Colt, he takes over the situation and guides me outside to his truck. Once inside, I shoot off a text and apologize to Mom and Dad for leaving them to handle the fallout. All I get back are a bunch of laughing emojis, so I can't help but laugh too.

We head toward the Dairy Queen just outside of town. Colt backs into a space at the far end of the parking lot, and we head inside to order. This is the place the farmers like to meet to talk ranch business. Blaze comes up to join them and get the news once a week or so.

It's also a popular spot on Sundays like this for the guys to hang out while the wives are at church. We get a few looks when we walk in but for the most part, the guys are friendly and smile or wave before returning to their conversations.

We step up to order, and Colt doesn't even flinch. He orders himself a Mint Chocolate

Chip Blizzard and me a Double Fudge Cookie Dough Blizzard. This has been our order for as long as I can remember. We would get these two, then share.

It started one night when we came out for ice cream, and I couldn't pick, so Colt ordered both. One for me and one for him so I didn't have to choose. It's just been our tradition ever since.

After we order, we head back to the truck and put the tailgate down to sit and eat our ice cream, overlooking the pasture behind the Dairy Queen with our backs to the building.

"You know, we did this for so long, even after you left, I found myself ordering Mint Chocolate Chip. It became my favorite because it was yours."

I smile at him. "I would buy a carton of both at the store and have a bowl with a scoop of each."

He laughed. We eat in silence for a few more minutes before he breaks the quiet.

"Thank you for standing up for me back there. Having you stand up for me..." He trails off and shakes his head. "I have no words."

I sigh. "One step at a time, Colt. Thank you for coming with me today. It means a lot."

"Well, I'll be by your side every week that you let me."

I look over at him and can't believe he's willing to go back after today. Why he would want to, is beyond me.

Like he can read my mind, he answers, "Dad does it for Mom, and I'll do it for you. They'll get used to me eventually, or they won't." He shrugs his shoulder. "Either way, I'll be there every Sunday with you." He leans over and gives me a chaste kiss and steals some of my ice cream.

We sit on the tailgate long after we finish our ice cream, just talking. We talk about the online schooling we did, the ranch, and funny memories growing up.

It may be Sunday, but that doesn't mean ranch work stops. Once we get home from Dairy Queen, I head to check on the horses, although I know Riley is already out there with them, and Colt heads to see if Blaze needs anything. I find Riley in the pen, working over a horse I bought a few months back. She was abused, and the owner was more than happy to trade her for money. She has been skittish but seems to have taken to Riley. Another month, and I think she'll be ready to ride.

Riley sees me and smiles. "Hey, how was church?"

"Fine until the potluck. Dorothy made a scene about Colt's *reputation*." I make air quotes with my fingers.

"She didn't!"

I nod. "She did, and I put her in her place. Colt dragged me out and took me for ice cream."

Riley laughed. "That man knows how to handle you." She pauses. "You're both happier now, ya know? We can all see it."

"Crap. I need to talk to everyone. I don't want to hide this anymore, and they don't know the story of what happened all those years ago," I say then shoot off a text to Colt.

Colt agrees we can talk to everyone tonight, so I shoot off a mass text to tell everyone to meet for dinner at the house. Mandatory attendance.

Chapter 10

Sage

Everyone is meeting at the house tonight, so I'm making fried chicken, biscuits, corn casserole, and a hot chocolate icebox cake for dessert. Yes, I'm buttering them up.

The cake has a dual purpose. If they are nice, they get cake. If they aren't, I withhold cake, and there's more for Colt and me to eat as we binge watch TV tonight.

Everyone is seated at the table and eating. When I say everyone, I mean everyone. Mom and Dad, Blaze and his fiancée Riley, Megan and her best friend (and why aren't they dating?), Hunter, Jason, Mac, and at my side Colt.

I look over at Colt, and he gives me an encouraging nod.

"Hey guys, I need to talk to you," I start.

All nine heads turn my way to hear what I have to say, and the room is eerily quiet.

"So, Colt and I have kept something from you guys, and I want you to let me talk. Then you can ask questions or get mad."

Everyone nods, but no one says a thing. I take a deep breath and look at Blaze.

"Remember when you asked me who my first kiss was, and I wouldn't tell you?"

He nods.

"It was Colt." I watch as Blaze's eyes flick to Colt then back to me. I don't get a read on him, but he stays quiet, so I keep going.

"The reason he always took me to all the school dances? It's because we were dating."

This time Blaze's eyes stay on Colt, and I see his jaw clench. He sits up straighter, glaring at Colt the whole time. Then he looks back at me.

"Colt and I knew from about the time he moved in with Mom and Dad that we were in love. We just didn't get what that meant. By our senior year of high school, we did. The night before graduation, we stayed up and talked."

I have to pause and take a deep breath before continuing.

Colt steps in, giving me a few minutes to collect myself.

"I knew then she was it for me. When I saw my future, it was all her. I had told her I loved her before, but I told her that night too." He looks over at me and takes my hand. "I told her she was my soulmate, and I couldn't live without her."

I pick up then. "My sperm donor used to say that to my egg donor, and I freaked out. That's why I left. I was scared, young, and stupid."

"Why didn't you tell us what was going on?" Blaze asks. His voice is soft and curious and not filled with the anger I had expected.

"The short answer is we were scared. I needed him. He helped with my nightmares when you couldn't. We feared what Mom and Dad would do if they found out. We feared what people in town would think. We were young, Blaze, and you know our history as much as we do. That stuff leaves scars, and it affects us."

No one says anything, so I continue. "I was planning to only be gone a few weeks. And what I'm about to say, I want you to know I in no way blame you. When you called and told me the rumors going around town of Colt without checking with him, those rumors kept me away."

I watch guilt cross his face. Then Colt speaks up.

"I would go to the bar with Jason and help him where I could. Cooking and cleaning, that sort of thing. A few months after Sage left, Dorothy's niece came in. She had just turned twenty-one, and she got drunk. Beyond wasted kind of drunk. Some trucker I had never seen before was pawing at her, and it didn't sit right with me. So, I took her home, laid her in her bed, fully clothed. I didn't even take off her shoes. I locked the door and came home. I didn't touch her, but the story got around that we left together. That's when the rumor mill started."

He pauses, and I squeeze his hand.

"A few weeks later, Sheila was home from college. Remember her? She was a few grades ahead of us in school?"

Blaze gives a short nod, and Colt continues.

"Again, she got drunk, and I took her home. Again, I didn't touch her, and I left. I kept praying if I did enough good, karma would protect Sage. I was worried and scared for her, and I needed her to be okay. Only once again, it backfired. The rumor mill kicked up and ran with it. Since both girls were no longer in town, I had no way to correct the stories. I didn't care, but I never for a minute thought you," He locks eyes with Blaze "would believe them without asking me."

Blaze looks like someone slapped him. Pure guilt on his face, but he keeps quiet.

"When I called to get the details of Megan's graduation, you told me Colt had been drinking and sleeping with a new girl every week."

I watch shame cross his face, and he looks down at the table. "I did say that." He nods. "I saw him leave with a girl. I heard the rumors, so I thought..." He hangs his head then.

Riley takes his hand but doesn't utter a word.

Colt picks the story back up. "A few weeks before Megan's graduation, I helped Kelli home. She had been drugged and was out of it bad. Nothing happened, but I stayed to make sure she was okay. I sat in a chair in the doorway all night. When she woke up, she thanked me, and I stayed for breakfast while the sheriff came over to file a report."

Jason chimes in, "I remember that. He talked to me and my staff on what we saw that night—who was there, who she was talking to."

"Well, after that, Kelli and I started hanging out at the bar. She would flirt, and I'd turn her down. Then the night Blaze told me Sage was coming back for Megan's graduation, I snuck some drinks at the bar." Colt cringes. "Sorry, Jason."

Jason just shakes his head, so Colt continues, "That night after a few drinks, I admitted to Kelli I was in love with Sage, and it would always be her."

Now, it was my turn to continue, "Well, I came home, and the day before the graduation, I ran into Kelli. She told me she and Colt were sleeping together, and they were in love."

"Which was a lie," Colt interrupts.

"Well, I couldn't stand it, so I left again," I say.

"When Sage left again, I was crushed. I was hurt, but Kelli was in my ear, and within a few days, I was just pissed. So, Kelli and I did start sleeping together. I had no idea until recently what Kelli had said to Sage before that. I put an end to it when Sage moved back. Then Sage and I both avoided each other. We were both hurt and mad at the other. But a few months before Riley showed up, I made the decision to fight for us. I just didn't have a plan. Then Riley showed up, and I put it on the back burner."

His grip on my hand tightens some. I give him a squeeze back, trying to give him my strength.

"All the emotions flared back up when Sage dated Brice. Then, there was the thing with Jed… I was so scared. I can't lose her. That night in the hospital after you all left, we talked. When we came home, I asked her to give me one month to date and to let us work all this out. So, that's what we're doing. We've been out on a few amazing dates."

He looks over at me and smiles. My heart flutters. I smile back so proud of him, admitting all this to them.

"And we've talked a lot," he continues. "There's a lot of hurt and misunderstandings to overcome, but we're talking."

"And part of that process is coming clean to all of you," I finish.

Everyone is silent and looking at Blaze, but it's Jason who speaks up first.

"I watched ya'll at the bar the other night. The way Colt looks at Sage… it's how Dad looks at Mom, and how Blaze looks at Riley. It's hot and intense. They both looked so happy. They danced after dinner and that kiss?" He laughs then looks at me "You had every woman in that room pissed because it wasn't them."

He pauses, and his eyes swing to Colt. "You two work this out, and Colt, you keep her happy. I'm okay with this."

I smile at him. "Thank you, Jason."

Mom and Dad look at each other, and Dad speaks next, "We always saw something there while you kids were growing up. We suspected it, but you're right. Things would have been different while you were living under our roof. I can't say what our reaction would have been then, but I can tell you what I said last night. If you're happy, we're happy."

Mom adds in, "I see Colt looking at you the way your father looks at me and vice versa. You treat each other well and work this shit out." My jaw drops. Mom never curses! "But if it doesn't work out, we aren't picking sides. You're both my kids, and I love you both. You *will* be at the dinner table every week together, regardless of what happens between you two. Do you understand?"

"Yes, Mom," Colt and I say at the same time, making her smile.

Mac speaks up next, "Sage, you know you have a special place in my heart after saving my life. I want nothing more than for you to be happy. You deserve it. If he doesn't treat you right, you let me know. I'll take care of him." He eyes Colt up.

I honestly don't know who would win that one. Mac may be younger than us by a few years, but he's all muscle.

I laugh though. "Thanks, Mac."

"I was always the odd man out," Megan says "And I get why. What you, Colt, and Mac went through as kids wasn't pretty. I thank you guys for shielding me. But because I was the odd man out, I got a different view of you guys. I saw the spark between you two back in high school, and I see it now. Work it out and don't be afraid to talk to us either. We're here for you both. But I agree with Mom. If this goes south, we aren't picking sides."

Hunter smiles at Megan then looks at me. "What she said." I laugh. Hunter will always have Megan's back.

That leaves Riley and Blaze, and I can tell Colt is just as nervous as I am because he squeezes my hand again. I see Riley looking at Blaze, and I can tell his mind is running, I guess Riley can too because she's next to speak.

"I know I'm the newest member of the family and what I say might not mean much, but I have talked to both of you. I'm happy you're working through this. You're both happier since you started talking again, so I'm happy for you."

My eyes tear up. "Riley, your opinion matters, and I'll kick anyone's ass who tells you it doesn't. That includes my brothers," I say and look at Blaze. The side of his mouth quirks up just a bit. He can act all tough, but he's told me before. He's happy I'm just as protective of Riley as he is.

Then the room is silent again as we all wait for Blaze to speak. My heart races. I don't know what I will do if Blaze isn't okay with this. Besides Colt, he has always been there for me, and he has been my best friend even longer.

Blaze looks at me and finally speaks, "Why didn't you talk to me? We talk about everything."

"At first, I was just scared. Then I was scared you would get mad we didn't talk to you first. The longer it went on, the more scared I was. Then there was Mom and Dad and what they would think. So, it was easier to hide it. It wasn't right, and I'm so sorry."

He nods, lost in thought. "You happy?"

"Yeah, I'm happy we're talking and hopeful for where it could go."

He nods again and then his gaze turns to Colt, and it goes ice cold.

"You're one of my best friends. You should have talked to me before it started." His tone is ice cold, one I've only heard very few times in my life.

Colt takes it in stride. "You're right, but it never really started. Yeah, we shared our first kiss, but there was never a starting point. It just happened. It was lunches out and alone time that turned into dates, and we never realized it. Our first makeout session led us to promising each other there was no one else. By that point, we were in deep."

I look over at Colt, and I can feel the blush creeping up my cheeks. That never happens. Then I look at Blaze, and he is looking between Colt and me.

"These guys may not pick sides," Blaze says, waving his arm around the table. "But I will. You hurt her? I *will* kick your ass, break a few bones, and send *your* ass to the hospital."

Colt squeezes my hand again. "If I screw this up, you can all take a turn kicking my ass."

That seems to satisfy Blaze. He nods and starts talking about the ranch. Everyone glances at me for a second and smiles. Then it's like it never happened. I take a deep breath, and my eyes lock with Colt's. He winks at me, and then we finish our dinner.

Chapter 11

Sage

Today, the girls are in Dallas to go dress shopping for Riley. Her whole wedding date is depending on finding a dress, so she sets up the first appointment and tells us all to make time. It's been a few days since the dinner where Colt and I told everyone about us, and things are still going well.

Today Riley had me, mom, Megan, and her friend Lilly here to help pick out dresses. This is the kind of place that pampers the bride to be and gives champagne out. Riley says she plans to spend the afternoon with us, so I'm kind of excited.

I guess Riley had been on the phone with the dress consultant because she has a few dresses pulled to try. They hang on a rack in the room we're brought to.

After we introduce ourselves, the dress consultant asks Riley what she is looking for in her dream dress.

"Well, I want something that is a little boho, a little country. I plan to wear cowgirl boots and I don't like tulle."

"Okay, I have a few dresses pulled from talking to you on the phone. I'd like all of you to look around and pull a few dresses you think Riley would like, then you can peek through and decide what to try on."

We all walk through the store and thirty minutes later, Riley is trying on her first dress. She steps out and while she looks beautiful, I know this isn't the dress, but I want to see what she says. She steps up in front of a three-way mirror and looks herself over.

"What do you guys think?" she asks.

No one says anything, so I speak up, "I can tell by your face it isn't the dress."

"No, it's not."

This process repeats but when she steps out in the sixth dress, my jaw drops. I watch her face light up as she looks in the mirror.

"Oh Riley, that's the dress. You look stunning," Mom says.

The dress consultant takes her cue and gets a veil to place on Riley, and I look her over. She's in an A-line dress made of chiffon with a ruched, off the shoulder, short sleeves. While it's floor-length, there are different layers to the bottom of the dress. It's very flowy and completely Riley.

"Who picked this one out?" the dress lady asks.

"That was me," Lilly says, and I watch Riley's eyes water.

"It's perfect. The girl who gave me the start to a new life, picked the dress to start it in. Sage, take my phone and get a few pictures, please."

I decide to text Blaze.

Me: Your girl found her dress. Blaze, she looks stunning.

Blaze: God, I can't wait to marry her. When will the dress be ready?

I listen in to the conversation between the dress girl and my mom, who insists on buying the dress for Riley. The dress needs a few alterations, but it will be ready in about three weeks.

Me: Four weeks. But, Blaze, this girl has been through a lot. I know you want to be married, but she's so happy today. Give in on this. Let her take some time and plan this wedding.

I see the three bubbles pop up and go away multiple times before his response comes.

Blaze: You're right. I want her to be my wife so bad, but I want her to enjoy this too. I want it to be perfect.

Me: I promise to do everything I can to make your day perfect. You both deserve it.

Blaze: Thank you, Sage. You will get your day soon if the way Colt looks at you is any indication.

I can't help but smile.

Me: I hope so, but we're taking it slow.

Riley interrupts me, saying she wants to check out a few shops for some wedding décor while we're in the city, so we head out from store to store then decide to have dinner before driving back.

Since Mom has driven us, she is a bit hesitant to stay out too much later, but Lilly steps in, offering to drive home since she drives these roads all the time being a truck driver. We agree. I decide to spoil Riley and take everyone to dinner at the Reunion Tower Restaurant owned by Wolfgang Puck. It has a bird's-eye view of the city, and the food is amazing.

Everyone is excited as I use an app to get us a table, and we're seated right away. I expect the conversation to go to Riley and the wedding, so I'm shocked when Riley asks about Colt.

"So, how are things with Colt?" Riley asks.

I smile. "Good."

"Come on, it's girls night. Give us more than that," Mom says.

"He was an amazing teenager, but as a man... Wow. He isn't the unsure boy figuring things out as we go anymore. He's this man who knows what he wants and won't let anything stop him from getting it. He's protective and strong, but he still remembers my favorite ice cream and how I like extra gravy on my meatloaf."

I shake my head and look around the table. Everyone is smiling. "You're in love," Mom says.

I look down at my lap. "I've always been in love with him. It never went away. I was just able to shove it behind a locked door. Now, he's back, always there, always touching me. I can't hide it anymore. I don't want to. I'm still scared, still second guessing myself sometimes. But I'm not running again."

They all nod. “Have you, ya know?” Lilly asks.

Mom covers her ears and hums, looking out the window. I laugh. “No, not this time. He’s been very adamant at taking things slow and telling me he wants me to know this isn’t about sex; it’s about us.”

“He’s one of the good ones,” Lilly says.

“He is,” I agree, and Megan taps Mom’s shoulder. She looks around the table.

“There are some things a mom just doesn’t need to know.”

We all laugh then fall into easy conversation about Riley’s wedding. My family is expanding, and I couldn’t be happier.

Chapter 12

Colt

Eight Years Ago

Sage and I've been mending a broken fence on the far side of the ranch with a rainstorm comes out of nowhere. It happens quite often this time of year; it's one of the reasons we have the cabins out here.

Unfortunately, by the time we get to the closest cabin, we're both soaked. We put the horses in the pen next to the cabin and run inside.

We burst through the door, and Sage laughs so hard, I can't help but laugh too. It's late fall, and I know if we don't get out of these wet clothes, we'll get sick.

"Why don't you call the main house and let them know where we are. I'll start a fire so we can get our clothes dry," I tell her.

She nods and heads to the small kitchen area to call Mom and Dad. The cabins are primitive. A fireplace for heating, one bedroom, and a bunch of sleeping bags in the closet, if needed. Basic nonperishable food that we stock up every three months and a bathroom that on a good day, you might get some warm water.

Once the fire is going, I stand to take off my boots and look back at Sage. She walks in and takes her boots off too.

"We need to get out of our wet clothes," I say, suddenly nervous. I've seen Sage in a bikini but for some reason, seeing her in her bra and underwear feels so much different.

She looks at me and nods. "Let me see what I can find." She walks into the bedroom and comes back out with a pair of sweatpants and a t-shirt.

"This is all that's here." She hands me the pants, and we get undressed, hanging our clothes by the fire to dry.

My mouth goes dry watching Sage peel off her shirt, leaving her in just her lacey bra. Then she takes her jeans off and turns her back to me while removing her bra and slipping the shirt over her head.

Oh Lord, help me now. I'm in so much trouble. When she turns, she smiles with a faint blush on her cheeks. I'm nervous too, but I can't hide how she affects me much longer.

"You're beautiful, Sage," I say in a gruff whisper.

She looks down at her feet, and the blush on her cheeks deepens. I love that I'm the only one who seems to get her to blush. That sexy look is just for me.

"Your turn," she says with heat in her eyes. I take off my shirt and jeans. Knowing my boxer briefs are next, I take a page from her book and turn my back to her to remove them. As I peel them off, I hear a sharp intake of breath from her. I have to start thinking of baseball stats while I pull on the sweatpants, but even the pants can't help hide how hard I am.

The thought of Sage in the sexy lace bra keeps running through my mind, and my dick is hard as nails once again.

We sit on the couch and before I can think twice, I'm kissing her. It's my favorite thing to do but when she climbs into my lap and straddles me, all I can think about is her and how she only has panties on under her shirt.

I tangle my hands in her hair and pull her toward me, deepening the kiss. She grinds against me, causing me to groan. She has me so worked up already, I don't think I'll survive if she keeps grinding on me like that.

She wraps her arms around my neck and flattens her chest against mine. Even though she has a shirt on, I can still feel the stiff peaks of her nipples rubbing against my chest.

I move my hands to her hips, over the shirt, and help her grind against me, watching the pleasure on her face. I've made Sage come before, many times; her face when she lets go is the sexiest thing I've ever seen.

To know I can give her that kind of pleasure turns me into a caveman and makes me want to beat on my chest.

Colt please woman. Made woman come.

I shift my hips just a bit to hit Sage's clit just right, and she tosses her head back and screams my name as she comes. I'm lost in the sight of the flush creeping up her chest and neck and her grip on my shoulders.

She rolls her head forward and looks at me with hooded eyes and then moves to stand. All I can do is watch her. She kneels on the ground in front of me and reaches for my pants.

"No, baby, this was about you."

"Please, Colt? I want to so badly." She moans, and I can never tell my girl no.

I swallow hard, give a short nod, and move my hands. She pulls the pants down, and my cock springs free, jumping out to greet her. She smiles and reaches out to stroke my cock. I could come right now.

I fist the cushions on the couch beside me as she lowers her head and takes me in her mouth.

"Fuck!" I say, and it takes everything in me not to thrust further into her mouth. The sight of Sage on her knees with my cock in her mouth, with the post-orgasm glow I gave her will be seared into my head for as long as I live.

I feel myself hit the back of her throat, and my hips jerk on their own. I toss my head against the back of the couch and tangle my hands in her hair. The feel of her tongue as it slides up and down my cock feels like heaven.

When I look back down and see myself slide between her lips, and her eyes lock with mine, I barely have time to give her a warning.

"Gonna... come," I groan, and she takes me to the back of her throat. I come so hard I can't catch my breath.

When she has milked the last drop from me, she kisses her way up my stomach before her mouth lands on me, and she straddles my lap again. She's leaning on me, chest to chest, with her arms wrapped around my neck and lazily kissing me.

We're in no rush to stop. I rub my hands up her back and tangle them in her hair. In no time, I am hard again. She grinds against me, feeling my hard cock, and I sense the smile in her kiss.

"Make love to me, Colt," she whispers against my lips.

"Sage..." I whisper back. "God, I want to so bad, but this is a huge step. It will be our first time, for both of us." I knew this was coming. I did my research. I wanted to make sure it was good for Sage when the time came. I was just thinking it would be prom night or next summer, not now.

"I want you, Colt. I want us." I swallow and nod. I carry her to the bedroom and lay her on the bed.

I check the nightstand and sure enough, there are condoms. I look back at Sage and take another deep breath.

"Shirt off, baby girl," I say barely above a whisper, and she takes it off, land on the floor as she lays back.

"God, I've never seen anything so perfect," I say and watch her as a light blush crosses her cheeks.

My eyes land on the circle bullet scar on her shoulder. A reminder of how close I came to losing her. A reminder about the promise I made myself of not letting a day go by where I don't tell her how I feel, how much I love her. I promised not to let a day go by where I don't take care of her and show her what she means to me.

I lean down and press my lips to that scar and run my tongue over it.

"Colt," she whispers. I look up and see a tear running down her face. I kiss it away then move back to the scar. I kiss it a few more times before I kiss down her chest and take her nipple in my mouth and make love to it with my tongue, then do the same with the other one.

I kiss down her stomach and pull her underwear down her legs. It joins the shirt on the floor.

I pull her legs apart as I lean in and lick her pussy from the slit to the clit, causing her hips to jerk. Sage gasps my name. I look up at her, and her eyes are on me wide and full of heat.

I latch on to her clit and suck while I thrust a finger into her. She's so tight, but I know I need to stretch her out before I'm inside her. After a minute, I add in a second finger and hook them to find the spongy spot inside her. She comes apart for me. I lick up her orgasm before kissing my way up her body.

I reach for the condoms, shed my pants, and roll a condom on. When I'm resting on top of her, I ask her again, "Are you sure?" I see nothing but love in her eyes.

"Yes, Colt, I want this. I need you so bad." That statement melts the last of my reserve.

I place my cock at her entrance, and she's so warm and wet. I ease inside her slowly. I'm only an inch in when I swear I could come, she feels so good.

I slide in a bit more before I feel her barrier reminding me I'm her first, like she's mine. I rest my forehead on hers.

"I hate this is going to hurt you, baby, but will you trust me to make it good for you?"

She wraps her arms around my neck. "I trust you, Colt. Always have, always will."

I nod and pull out, then give a solid thrust forward into her, and I feel the barrier give away. I feel her clamp down around me. She lets out a small squeal of pain, and I hold myself still in her trying to let her adjust. I kiss her mouth, her jaw, her neck, her ear, and tell her how good she feels and how perfect she is.

"Oh God, Colt, I need you to move," she says as she wiggles her hips.

I pull back and thrust in slowly and gently.

"How does that feel, baby?" I ask.

"So good," she groans.

I slowly pick up the pace and reach between us to strum her clit. I know I won't last long, and I need her to come again.

When I feel her pussy clamp down on my cock, she screams my name. I come harder than I ever had in my life. I've never felt anything so good and never thought it could be like this.

I roll to the side once we both relax, and I kiss her slowly.

"That was amazing," she says, and I smile.

"I agree." I get up and take care of the condom then grab a washcloth to clean her up before getting back in bed with her.

We drift off to sleep, but I wake up a while later with her mouth on my cock. When I groan, she looks up at me.

"I need you again, Colt," she says.

"Baby, you have to be sore." She shakes her head. I grab another condom, pull her hips on mine, and let her ride me, and lead the show this time.

The storm goes on all night, and we make love two more times before heading back to the house the next morning.

Chapter 13

Sage

Later that week, there's a lull in my horse clients. My current horse just went home, and my next one doesn't arrive until Monday. After doing some paperwork, I hunt down Colt.

I'm dressed casually in jeans ripped at the knees and a red t-shirt that says, "Howdy" with a cactus on it. I have on my work cowboy boots and a cowboy hat on.

I find Colt over on Blaze's side of the ranch behind the barn. He doesn't see me right away, so I stand back and take him in.

He's in a pair of work jeans, well-worn with stains on them. He has on a blue cowboy shirt, cowboy boots, and a cowboy hat. What has my mouth watering are the brown leather chaps he's wearing as he's leaning against the fence.

I pull out my phone and snap a few photos. This is one memory I don't want to forget. I slide my phone back in my pocket before heading over.

"Hey," I call out to him and watch him turn to me. A huge smile takes over his face.

"I'm going to head out and run some fences on the back forty. Want to come with me?" I ask.

"Yeah, give me ten minutes?" he asks.

I nod. "Meet you in the barn."

It's been a while since I've checked the fences back there myself. I know the ranch hands have done it, but I like to see it myself too. I know the condition they're in. Dad has always been very adamant about being hands-on and seeing things for himself. He has drilled that into us as well.

I get my horse and Colt's saddled up, and we head out. We talk about some of the plans we're looking to make this coming year for the ranch and our plan for Hell Week coming up.

Hell Week comes around twice a year, in the spring and fall. We're up from sunup to sundown, checking cattle, doing preggo checks, vaccinations, making sure there's enough hay for the winter, and winterizing the ranch. In the spring, we prep the ranch for the warmer months, do tractor maintenance and do some checks on the cattle. In the spring, we also separate cattle we plan to sell and move pastures around.

This takes at least seven days, but if we're shorthanded, it has been known to last as long as fourteen days. Those are the worst, but we band together to get it done.

It takes all hands on deck, and we even get a few guys from the reservation to help. Megan takes over cooking since she gets home from the salon early that week. Jason helps during the week too, and so does Hunter, as his classes allow.

We run the back fence, and it looks good. Then I notice where we are. Out by our cabin, I look up to see Colt has noticed too. Without a word, we make our way to the cabin and tie the horses up in the shade.

No sooner are we inside the cabin, does he have me pinned up against the door with his lips on mine.

He has one hand at the back of my neck, pulling me into him. The other hand is on my hip, pinning me to the door. The hand at my neck glides down over my shoulder, over my breasts, and rests on my hip.

I wrap my arms around his neck and deepen this kiss with a moan. He presses into me even more, and I can feel him hard and ready for me, pressing into my stomach.

His hands reach down to cup my ass, and I take the opportunity to wrap my legs around his waist which causes him to groan.

"Sage..." he whispers against my lips.

"This is our cabin, Colt," I whisper.

"Sage, I want you so bad," he groans.

"Then take me. I'm yours, I always have been."

He pulls back to look me in the eye. "I need you to understand what this means."

He kisses my neck. "Once I'm inside you again, Sage, you're mine. I'm not letting you go again. Things will be scary. We will fight, but we will do it together. If you run, I will chase you because. You. Are. Mine. If you need more time, I'll give you all the time in the world, Sage. Once we cross this line, there's no going back."

Since that kiss the night in his truck under the stars, there has been no going back for me. What we felt all those years ago was strong, but what I feel now? It's earth shattering. There's no going back. There's no walking away.

I am his. I've always been his. I will always be his.

Am I scared? Yes, but being scared isn't a reason to stop you from taking the leap. The best things in life aren't easy. For most of them, you will be scared to do, try, or say.

So yes, I'm scared to trust Colt again, to be us again, but that means that it's going to be worth it coming out on the other side.

"I'm yours, Colt. This also means you're mine. Only mine."

"Sage, Sage, Sage, I've only ever been yours. There's no one else for me. I love you with everything I am, and I'm not going anywhere."

My heart races. It's the first time I've heard those words in years. I soak them in and let them heal me.

"I love you too, Colt."

With that, he moves from the door to the small bedroom and places me on the bed. We remove our boots before he turns back to kiss me gently and then reaches for my shirt. He looks me in the eyes, making sure it's okay. I nod, and he removes my shirt.

He takes in my lace bra and runs his thumbs over my breasts, causing my nipples to harden even further.

"You're the most beautiful woman I've ever seen." He reaches behind him and pulls his shirt off. Holy mother of cowboy abs, there's a reason everyone loves cowboys. The hard, manual labor gives them a body that I just want to sink my teeth into.

I push him back on the bed and stare.

"Your body is definitely different," I say, running a finger over each ab. Then I trace the tattoo over his heart. It's a heart covered in sage leaves. My eyes lock with his.

"When did you get this?" I ask, still tracing my finger over it.

"A few weeks after you left the first time."

I move to look at the tattoo on his arm. To anyone else, it looks like a collage of places from around the ranch. To me, I know exactly what it is, and it makes my eyes water. It's the barn where he saw me for the first time, the church where he told me he loved me the first time, the graveyard where we kissed for the first time, the wagon tracks from our first date, the creek from our first makeout session, and the cabin from where we made love the first time.

I trace my finger over each one. "When did you get this one?" I must know.

"A week after Megan's graduation."

The tears roll down my face; I can't stop them. He wraps his arms around me and pulls me down to the bed next to him. Then wipes my tears.

"It's always been you, Sage," he whispers.

I can't get the words out, so I lean up and kiss him. Then I lean down and run my tongue over the ridges of his abs. He tosses his head back and moans.

He groans my name a few times before grabbing my hips and flipping me over. He reaches behind me and unhooks my bra. Instead of going for my breast, his lips land on the circle bullet scar on my shoulder.

I'm instantly back to our first time, in this bed, his lips on that scar. He runs his tongue over the scarred flesh, and it causes my whole body to shiver.

Then he moves to the new scar, the straight line from the knife. He kisses along it, so sweet he brings tears to my eyes. When he looks up and sees the tears, he kisses the corner of my eyes.

He slides my pants and panties down until I am bare to him. He pulls my legs open wide and stares at my glistening pussy lips. He moves his mouth to cover my clit and sucks firmly, causing my hips to buck.

I feel his smile on my pussy, proud he still remembers my body so well. As his tongue continues its assault on my tight bundle of nerves, he inserts his middle finger and strokes me before adding a second finger. After a few more strokes, he hooks them, finding that perfect spot inside me that causes me to shatter and fall apart, screaming his name.

He sits up looking at me before he stands and takes off his pants and boxer briefs. He goes to the nightstand for a condom.

"Shit."

"What?" I ask, concerned.

"No condoms."

I grab his hand. "I'm clean, and I'm on the pill. Have been for years."

He closes his eyes. "I'm clean too. The paperwork is in my room." Then he climbs on the bed and settles over me. "Why are you on the pill, love?"

I know he's wondering because I had told him it's been years since I've been with anyone.

"It helps with my periods." He nods then frames my face with his hands. "I'd love nothing more than to take you bare. I've never done that before, but I want it with you. Are you sure?"

"Yes, Colt. I've never done it either, but I want to with you."

He leans down to kiss me, all gentle and sweet, then looks up at me. Never breaking eye contact, he slides into me, only pausing once he's fully set inside me.

"Colt..."

"Fuck, Sage. You feel so damn good," he says as he thrusts.

He reaches down and strokes my clit. "I'm not going to last very much longer. I need you to come," he grunts out.

He angles his hips and thrusts harder. His mouth kisses down to the spot below my ear, and he nips me there, causing me to climax again. A few more thrusts and he joins me.

He rolls to his side, taking me with him so we don't lose the connection. Then he kisses me so tenderly.

"I love you, Sage. This is it. This is us. Forever."

"I love you too, Colt. Forever"

I rest my head on his shoulder. "Seems fitting."

He laughs. "That our first time after all these years is where we had sex the first time back then?"

I smile. "Exactly."

He kisses the top of my head. "I agree."

After a few more minutes, he asks, "So, does this mean you'll sleep in my bed with me tonight?"

I smile. "No." I watch his face crumble. "But you can sleep in mine." And he smiles again.

Chapter 14

Colt

It's been a week since our time in the cabin, and I can't remember the last time I've been this happy. I get to wake up every morning with Sage in my arms, and I get to start my day inside her. We get up and shower together then head down to breakfast.

After breakfast, we go our own ways on the ranch, sometimes meeting up for lunch. After dinner, we go for walks and talk about everything and anything.

We've talked a lot about the past and our feelings and how we hurt each other. We've worked out several misunderstandings and talked about how we should have handled it and how we would handle things in the future.

We've had many talks about our plans as well as where we see us going and how we'd be as a family. When that topic came up, I don't think I can keep the smile from my face.

Picturing Sage round with my child and us starting a family that we've both always so desperately wanted.

After our walks, we come in and watch TV. I get to spend every night in bed with her and fall asleep with her in my arms.

This is how I always pictured our life when we were making plans for our future. This is the life I want. If I thought Sage would say yes, I'd ask her to marry me today and then run off to Vegas to make her mine.

I know Sage though. When I do pop the question, I don't want any doubt in her mind about us. I want to give her the big romantic proposal she deserves and the wedding she has always dreamed of.

I look over at Sage, still asleep with her hair fanned out on her pillow. She looks like an angel. I've always thought so. Back when she had all her nightmares, and I'd be in bed with her, I wouldn't sleep much. I would be up watching her sleep. She would catch me a lot and just smile and snuggle in closer to me.

I lightly move the hair out of her face, and it causes her to stir. She blinks, opens her eyes, and smiles at me. This makes my heart clench every time. My Sage is so *not* a morning person; having her wake up and smile at me makes me feel ten feet tall.

"Did you sleep at all?" she asks me, and I can't help but smile and kiss her forehead.

"Yes, I woke up about ten minutes ago."

Sage doesn't move; she keeps watching me then slowly brings her hand up to my face. I close my eyes and soak up her touch. It has healing powers, I swear it does. When I open my eyes again and look at her; the look of love and passion in her eyes takes my breath away.

"I love you, Colton. I don't know how you've managed to do it, but you've healed by heart and managed to steal it all over again. I love seeing the little things you do for me to show you love me. I love hearing it when you say it. I love starting and ending every day with you, and I love the future we have planned."

I can't stop my eyes from misting over. "I love you too, Sage. I'm not me without you, and I don't ever want to be without you again."

I lean in and kiss her as we ignore the alarm clock and make love soft and sweet that morning. By the time we get downstairs, everyone is already gone.

I know what I need to do today, so I head off to find Blaze on the east side of the ranch, saddling up a horse at the barn.

"Late start today, huh?" he jokes.

I smile. "What are you up to today?"

"Riding out to check a few pastures. We need to move the Delta cattle herd next week. I also want to check the fences."

"Want some company?" He looks me over and then nods.

I saddle up my horse, grab some supplies, and off we go.

I can't help but notice the difference just a few weeks can make. Before Sage and I started talking again, I would love the monotony of ranch work like this. You can zone out, and it's quiet. I used to love that. No one out here to bug me.

This is where I'd come to think. I'd do my job and before I knew it, it would be dinner time. Days would fly by, and I'd look forward to the next time I could get out in the fields again.

Now, not so much. I'd rather be by Sage's side, watching her, listening to her talk and laugh. I now hate being all the way out here and away from her. Time seems to drag on.

Even when I try to put her out of my mind to focus on what I want to talk to Blaze about, she's right back there, taking over. What is she doing? Is she thinking of me? Can I get back and pull her into the barn office and bend her over the desk?

Shit, I need to get my mind off Sage. Riding a horse with a hard on isn't the most comfortable thing in the world.

We're silent for the first twenty minutes before Blaze speaks, "What's on your mind, Colt? I know you aren't out here for my bubbly personality."

I shake my head and take a deep breath. I just need to say it, "I want to ask Sage to marry me."

Blaze is silent. "Have you guys worked through your shit?"

"Yeah, we've been talking nightly. What we should have done differently, what we'll do from now on. She's always been the one, and it doesn't matter if it's now or ten years from now. I'm going to do everything possible to make her happy and marry her."

We cross the creek, and I continue, "I know we hurt you keeping this a secret, and I'm sorry for that. I want you to know I came to you first. I haven't talked to anyone else about this. I need you and me, and you and Sage to be okay before moving forward."

He sighs. "Sage came to me last week. We had lunch and talked it all out. She cried, and I gave my blessing to all this. I think she cried on purpose, but I can't prove it," he grumbles. "You two are my best friends, and I hate that you hid this from me but so long as you promise not to do it again, and you make her happy, I'm okay with it. But I still stand by Sage. If you hurt her, I'll kick your ass. I've spent my life keeping people from hurting her, and that includes you."

I smile. "Good. She needs you. I swear it. I'll go to my grave doing everything possible to make her happy."

He nods. "I forgive you guys, but I still reserve the right to bring it up and pick on it anytime I want." He smiles.

"Understood."

"You'll be my best man. If I have to suffer Riley and Sage's wedding planning twice, so do you."

With that, I laugh. "I wouldn't have it any other way. Please keep this between us. I'm going to talk to Mom and Dad tonight, the guys tomorrow, and Riley and Megan last. Those two can't keep secrets."

"I don't keep secrets from Riley..." He pauses. "Make sure you talk to her tomorrow, or I will."

"Deal."

Heading back to the ranch, I stop at the graveyard. Mom and Dad told me as soon as they knew both of my parents were dead, they were adopting me. It was never a question. For that reason, they asked if I wanted my mom buried in the family graveyard here at the ranch, and I agreed.

I tie my horse to the fence before heading through the gate toward the front right corner under the cedar elm tree. I sit next to my mom, take a deep breath, and let it all pour out. I tell her about everything going on with Sage from the time she was in the hospital until now.

It's calming to tell my mom, and I feel bad. I should be out here more.

"Mom, I'm going to ask Sage to marry me. I know you always liked her. I wish you were here to help her pick her wedding dress and stand by me for photos. Sage will want to get married at the ranch church here on the property, I know it. We'll give you the grandkids you always wanted, and I promise to bring them here. We can do afternoon picnics as I tell them stories of their grandma who watches over them."

My eyes tear up. Mom always did the best she could to protect me and take care of me. So many times, she went without, so I had what I needed. I always wanted to grow up and take care of her. That was the plan, but best laid plans and all that.

I spend another half hour talking to her before heading back to the house for lunch.

After lunch, I head over to Mom and Dad's house. I enter via the kitchen and instantly smell her homemade banana bread. It's my favorite, and it makes my mouth water, even though I had had Sage's baked mac and cheese for lunch.

I walk up behind Mom and give her a hug.

"Hey, Mom."

"Hey, baby. Everything okay?"

"Yeah, can I talk to you and Dad about something?"

She wipes her hands on her apron and turns around to study my face.

"Of course, baby. Your father is in his study. Head on in and let me clean up. I'll be just a minute."

I head into Dad's study, and even though the door is open, I knock on the doorframe.

He has always had an open-door policy for us kids. We're free to come and go from the study. He has never hidden anything from us. No matter how many times he tells me I don't have to knock, I still feel like I need to.

His study commands authority and attention. When you walk in, there's a large window on the back wall that looks out over the barn, so he can watch the ranch hands from his office. Sage loved the idea so much, she set up her office at the house the same way.

The windows let in a lot of light, so the study is always bright, but it has dark-wood walls lined with bookcases filled with books. Lots of books on the history of the area and the ranch. Many journals from the family and tons of ranching books.

All of us kids loved being in here reading them, especially Sage. That thought brings a smile to my face. Dad has a large wood desk, the kind you picture in any large office; he uses it mostly used for storage.

In one corner of the room, we have had many talks in a comfortable sitting area. We would come in, sit, and read while he did the bookwork.

Dad looks up when he hears me knock and smiles at me.

"Hey son, come on in. Did you stop in and see Mom already?"

"Yeah, she'll be here in a minute. I was hoping to talk to you both."

I watch Dad's face fall just a bit. "Is everything okay?"

"Yeah, it's good news, I hope. I hope you'll take it that way anyway," I say, getting nervous.

Dad stands from behind his large wooden desk and sits in one of the armchairs in the little seating area with the couch and a second armchair. This is the same seating area mom and dad would have many talks with us kids growing up and My nerves are now getting the best of me.

Mom walks in and closes the door. I take a seat on the couch and Mom sits in the other armchair. I watch Dad look at Mom like she hung the moon. He reaches over and takes her hand in his before giving me his attention. I have a brief glimpse of moments like this with Sage and our own kids one day.

I rest my arms on my legs, rub my hands together, and take a deep breath. Then I look up and look Dad in the eye like he taught me.

"Sage and I've been working things out. We've been talking every night, and we're in a good place. A better place than when we were eighteen. We aren't hiding us from anyone anymore." I pause. They are watching me, so I take a deep breath.

"I love her. I have for as long as I can remember. I think I fell in love when I first saw her in the barn when we were six. I think I realized it when we sat on my front porch after she saved my life when we were fourteen, and I knew I'd never let her go when I sat by her hospital bed after she saved Mac's life when we were sixteen. She's it for me, and I want to ask her to marry me."

There, I've said it. I look at Mom first, and I see tears in her eyes. I look at Dad, and he seems... proud. Without a word, Dad walks over to the hidden safe in the bookcase. He pulls out a small box and closes the safe before sitting back down.

"After Sage came to us, I watched her bio mother and every move she made. I didn't trust her. She sold off anything of value, trying to hold onto the property. She sold a bunch of jewelry, and I picked this up." He hands me the box, and I open it.

It's an antique wedding and engagement ring and a matching men's wedding ring. The engagement ring is stunning, and I know I've seen it before. It's white gold, which I know Sage loves, with a large diamond in the center and three smaller diamonds on either side in a swirl design.

I look up at Dad, and I can tell he sees the question in my eyes.

"This was Sage's grandmother's wedding set and her grandfather's wedding band."

I take a deep breath. Sage loved her grandparents. They died when she was eight, only a few months apart from each other in a nursing home a few towns over. Mom and Dad took Blaze, Sage, and me many times to see them on the weekends. Then we would go out for lunch and ice cream or catch a movie. That's why the ring looks familiar.

Tears well up in my eyes. "Thank you." My voice is husky with emotion.

"We've seen how you two are together. We've watched, and I can tell how much you love each other. Honestly, the day you showed up at church with her, I knew this day was coming. You treat her right. Marriage isn't easy. There will be hard times but don't give up, and don't walk away. She kicks you out?

Sleep on the couch in your room. Put as little space between you as possible. We're always here if you need advice, but I'm so happy for you both," Dad says and then stands to hug me.

Mom hugs me next, but then she pulls back to look me in the eyes, keeping her hands on my shoulders.

"That day Sage went to your house and... everything happened. When I showed up and saw you two huddled on the front porch together, I knew. I knew in my heart then you two were meant to be. I love you both. You share a bond no one else does, but you will have to work on it every day." She leans in and hugs me again.

"Now, any special plans on this proposal?" she asks.

"Not yet. I talked to Blaze first, but I still need to talk to the guys and Megan and Riley. I think I want to do something that includes all of them."

"I have an idea, if you're interested," Mom says with a twinkle in her eyes. Dad and I laugh.

We make plans over some sweet tea and fresh banana bread before I head out to find the guys.

Chapter 15

Colt

After my time making plans with Mom, I head out to find Jason before he heads to the bar. I catch him in the kitchen and take him to the barn office and close the door. When I tell him my plan to propose to Sage, he's all excited and wants to know what he can do to help. I tell him I will let him know.

Next, I track down Mac in the barn. He's just as excited as I am.

"About damn time, man," he says. "Ever since I've known you two, I knew you two belonged together. I like seeing you both happy."

Now the girls. I had planned to wait until tomorrow to talk to them, but I know Blaze hates keeping things from Riley. It's how I feel at the thought of keeping something from Sage. So, I figure I'll do it today and cut him some slack.

Megan is at the hair salon she owns in town, and I don't have time to meet her before dinner. I decide to do a video call with her. The bonus is I can skip the strong hair salon smell.

"Hey Colt, what's wrong?" she answers the call.

"Nothing. Can you go somewhere private? I don't need the town gossips in on this." She laughs and heads to the back room.

"Okay, I'm in the storage room, but I can't promise they don't have their ears to the door out there."

I sigh. "I want to ask Sage to marry me."

She has no emotion on her face. "Okay....?"

"How do you feel about it?"

"Oh Colt, you don't need my permission. I love how happy you two are. What kind of sister and friend would I be to stand in the way of that?"

I smile. "Thanks, Megan. Mom and I have an idea for a proposal. Will you help?"

"Of course!"

"Okay. Head to Mom's when you get out of work. I still need to talk to Riley."

"Okay. Later, Colt."

"Later, Megs."

I hang up and look out the office window. Sage and Riley are working a horse out in the pen. How do I get Riley away from Sage without raising suspicions?

Blaze.

I head to the barn on the east side of the property and step into Blaze's barn office.

Me: Hey, I need to get Riley away from Sage. Can you ask her to meet you in your barn office?

Blaze: But I'm not there.

Me: No, I am. This way I can talk to her. Sage won't think twice about you asking her to come here.

A good minute goes by like he's thinking about it.

Me: Or else I will have to wait until tomorrow to talk to her.

Blaze: Fine.

Fifteen minutes later, Riley walks in.

"Oh, sorry. I was looking for Blaze."

"Actually, I asked him to text you. I wanted to talk to you but didn't want Sage to know."

She narrows her eyes at me.

"And why would that be?"

I smile. "I want to ask her to marry me."

Her face lights up, jumping up and down.

"Oh my God! Really?! Oh, finally. I can't wait!"

"Listen, it needs to be kept a secret. Mom and I came up with the epic proposal she deserves, and I need your help."

"Of course! What do you need?"

"After dinner, will you ask Blaze to go for a walk with you and then head over to Mom's and get the details from her?"

"You got it!"

We chat for a few more minutes. Then she heads back to help Sage. I can't keep the smile off my face.

Deciding I can't stay away from Sage anymore, I finally track her down. What I find stops me dead in my tracks.

Chapter 16

Sage

My mind races as I pack my bag in my room. I don't hear anyone come into the room until I hear Colt's voice.

"You have to be fucking kidding me."

I spin around, and all I see is anger on his face.

"Colt, listen..." I start, but he interrupts me.

"Were you even going to say goodbye this time? I'm shocked you're even leaving in daylight. Why not wait until night and leave another note?"

I close my eyes. I know how this looks, but it's not what he thinks. I take a deep breath. My instinct is to yell and let him think what he wants, but I know that will cause more hurt than anything. This isn't about him and me, and I need him to know that.

I calmly walk over to him and place my hand on his shoulders.

"Colt, look at me." I wait until his eyes meet mine. "I'm not leaving you."

"Then why the hell are you packing, Sage?!"

"Colt, take a deep breath and let me talk. I will tell you."

He pulls away from me and sits on the couch on the far side of my room. He rests his elbows on his knees and puts his head in his hands, running his hands through his hair.

I kneel on the floor in front of him and place my hands on his arms.

"My friend Abby just called. Her parents were in a car crash, and they didn't make it." I watch him look up, and his eyes meet mine. "She's an only child and has no other family. She was raised in a strict church and has expressed to me a few times that she doesn't want to be part of that church. She fears what the church might do now that she's alone. She was in tears, begging me to help her. So, that's what I'm doing. I'm going to help her bury her parents and get out of town. More than likely, I'll bring her here until she figures out her next steps."

He takes a deep breath and rests his forehead against mine, taking my face in his hands.

"I'm sorry I jumped to conclusions. When do you leave?"

I take his face in my hands. "It's okay, Colt. I know what it must have looked like walking in here. I get it. I'm packing and heading straight there. I'm going to drive through the night."

"Where does she live?"

"Tennessee, Memphis area."

"How long will you be gone?"

"I honestly don't know. A week maybe? But Colt..." I pull my head away from his and find his eyes. "I *am* coming back as soon as possible."

I can tell he's wary of this. We don't have good memories of me leaving town, and that's my fault. This isn't like last time.

I lean in and kiss him softly. "Come with me," I whisper against his lips.

"I can't... the ranch," he whispers back, sounding choked up. He knots his hands in my hair and pulls me to him for a hard, passionate kiss. His tongue finds mine and tangles, fighting for dominance.

When he pulls back, we're both breathless.

"We will talk every night," he says.

"And text all day. Video calls when I can. Colt, let me see your phone." He doesn't hesitate and hands it to me. I download an app and connect it. After a few minutes, I hand it to him.

"What's this?"

"This allows you to track me and see where I am. I'm not running from you, I swear it. I hope this gives you peace of mind."

He gives me a half smile. "Promise you'll hurry home to me?"

"I swear as fast as I possibly can. I need to finish packing. Will you call everyone and let them know please?"

He nods and pulls out his phone again while I finish packing. Not sure what I'll need, I reach to the back of the closet and pull out the black dress I wanted to burn the last time I had to see it.

Seven Years Ago

The clock on my car says one a.m. It feels wrong sneaking out of town in the middle of the night, but I can't face everyone to say goodbye. I know Colt wouldn't have let me go. He would demand answers I don't have.

At the thought of Colt, my heart squeezes. He's my best friend, my everything. So, why am I running? My sperm donor was my egg donor's everything, and he was an abusive asshole.

That's not Colt though. I know that, but it doesn't mean he doesn't have the power to hurt me in other ways.

Thanks for Visiting Rock Springs. Y'all Come Back Now!

The sign mocks me. Rock Springs has been my home my whole life. I love Mom and Dad. They took me in when I had no one. Then there are my brothers and Megan. I will miss them, but I'll be back for Megan's graduation next year at the latest. I think I just need a few weeks or so to get my head on straight and think.

I need to clear my head before I face Colt again. Come on, no one meets their soulmate at age six, right?

Right?

Do I believe in soulmates? I think so. How can I not? If what I feel with Colt isn't soulmates, then I don't know what it is. My heart hurts more with each mile between me and Rock Springs. Between me and Colt.

I can't think about all this, so I crank up the music and drive.

Welcome to Arkansas!

I stop at the rest stop and look at the map. I can be in Memphis by morning. I always wanted to see

Graceland. I smile and point my car east.

My heart may be broken, but my soul is finding peace on the open road, fulfilling my bucket list.

As I near Memphis, my phone goes off. Everyone is up and must have found my note. I can answer them all when I get in.

As I enter a town, I see signs for a cute bed and breakfast, and I pull in, hoping they have a room.

Grace is up and making breakfast. I tell her I had been driving all night, and she ushers me right up to my room. She tells me to come down whenever I am ready. She will save me some food.

I get in and settle on my bed. I've missed calls from everyone but Colt. No texts either. I send out a group text.

***Me:** I'm fine. I just pulled into a B&B for a few days. Call when I get some sleep.*

Then I close my eyes, praying I can sleep, and the nightmares will stay away now that there's space between me and that place.

Chapter 17

Sage

Thanks for Visiting Rock Springs. Y'all Come Back Now!

Leaving town this time is just as hard; knowing I'm leaving on good terms helps a little.

To calm my heart, I used the Bluetooth and call Colt.

"Hey, baby. Everything okay?"

"Yeah, just passed the leaving Rock Springs sign and had some flashbacks. I just needed to hear your voice. Remind myself this isn't like last time."

"Well, I'm always a phone call away, and I'll be here waiting when you get back. Just try to make it sooner rather than later."

I laugh.

"I just passed the city limits, and I'm wanting to turn around. I can promise there will be nothing stopping me from getting back to you."

"Tell me about Abby."

I smile. "The night I left, I drove all night, and my first stop was Memphis. I pulled in at daybreak and stopped at this cute little B&B. The lady who checked me in was Grace, Abby's mom. Her parents ran the B&B. I had planned to stay a few nights to see Graceland and explore a bit. Because of them, I stayed a month. Their housekeeper was on maternity leave, so I filled the spot and got my room and meals for free."

"You took many odd jobs on the road." I can hear the smile in Colt's voice.

"I wanted to save my money, so anytime I could work for my room, I took it. It's how I made so many friends. Abby is a sweet girl and an only child. Her parents have no family, so the B&B falls to her. But the church her family belonged to has super-strict rules. They don't think she can own the property without being married. From what I've learned, they will try to force her to marry. She wants out. Her parents were letting her find someone out of the church to marry. They would never force her, but the church will."

"Sage, is it going to be safe for you there?"

"I have a conceal and carry permit in Tennessee, and I brought my gun. It won't get that far, Colt. The church is used to a submissive woman. I scare them, and they don't want anything to do with me. Once I'm there, we will take care of everything, then pack her up and bring her home so she can plan her next steps on her own."

"What about the B&B?"

"Abby doesn't want to run it. It was her mom's dream, but she isn't interested. They have a few standing offers on it, so we'll look at closing it. Her parents were older and had everything set up to make this easy on Abby."

"What does Abby want to do?"

"She wants to be a midwife, and the church approved because she could be the church midwife. That's not what she wants. She wants out of the church and those rules, but she's still very conservative. I don't think she'll want to live on her own."

"Well, you know everyone will welcome her here."

"Yeah, and I'd love for her to stay, but I don't think she'll be happy here. She isn't a country girl. She likes people for the most part. I've been racking my brain. I know a family in Arkansas. They're a larger family and conservative like her, but they aren't strict. Their church is a good one. Once she gets settled, I'm thinking of taking her up there to see how they fit. Maybe she could stay with them. She'd be happier, I think."

There's a pause in the conversation before Colt speaks again.

"I miss you already, Sage."

"I miss you too, Colt. I plan to drive straight through. Can we video chat when I get in? It will be late though."

"Call me any time. I'll always answer. I always want to hear your voice and see you. I love you, Sage. You be careful."

"I love you too. And I promise I will."

When we hang up, I crank up the music and try to enjoy the drive on the open road as I used to all those years ago

I pull into the B&B around six a.m. and just take it all in. The memories of the first time I walked through that door, the fun and laughter that filled its walls, and the pain of walking away when I did.

I climb the steps to the large wraparound porch of the white 1850s home. That was the start of my journey all those years ago.

Before I even get the chance to get to the door, Abby meets me with a huge hug she and her mamma are famous for. It feels like home even though I haven't been here in years.

"Sage, I'm so glad you're here. I didn't know who else to call."

I hug her back just as tight. "Well, I'm here, and we'll get through this. I think time is a factor. The quicker we can take care of everything and get you back to the ranch, the better. You can mourn there, okay?"

She nods. "I've been so scared, I haven't had time to mourn."

"We need to look at their will and what legal rights we have. The biggest thing will be to get this place sold. You sure you still want to do that?"

"I love this place, but yes, I have no interest in running it. The couple I want to sell too had their honeymoon here and have returned once or twice a year. They love the place as much as my mom did. More than I do. They'll be here tomorrow."

"Perfect. Let's get inside. I need to let my family know I made it, and I need a few hours of sleep."

"I thought maybe you would share my room again?"

I smile. "I'd love to. I know I wouldn't want to be alone."

She gets me set up, and I get ready to sleep for a bit and do a video call to Colt.

"Hey, you make it in okay?" he answers in a groggy voice. He's still lying in bed and looks sexy as hell with his sleepy face and hair tousled. It sends a jolt south seeing him like this. My panties are soaked instantly.

What I wouldn't give to be there with him right now and wrap my arms around him and pull him on top of me...

I need to stop this train of thought. It won't make my time here any easier, and it's making me miss him even more. It hasn't even been twenty-four hours yet.

"Yeah. I talked with Abby a little and just got to my bed. I'll be catching just a few hours of sleep when we get off the phone."

"I couldn't sleep without you here. I tried to sleep in my own bed but gave up and came to your room. You don't mind, do you?"

I groan. "Thinking of you in my bed will make it even harder to sleep. But, Colt, wouldn't you say that it's our bed now?"

His smile lights up his whole face. "Damn right it is." Then I watch his face grow with heat. "What are you wearing, baby?"

I laugh. "Nothing sexy." I pan the phone down. I'm in one of his shirts and a pair of sleep shorts.

"You look damn good in my shirt."

I laugh. "I miss you, Colt."

"I miss you too, Sage. I should have gone with you. I didn't think it would be this hard."

"We meet with Abby's parents' attorney later today, and the couple that wants to buy the B&B will be in tomorrow. We need to make funeral arrangements, and I will text you soon as I know anything."

"Okay, call me before bed?"

"Video call, I promise."

"Love you, Sage. Be safe."

"Love you to, Colt. I will be."

Despite how much I miss Colt, sleep pulls me under soon as I close my eyes.

Chapter 18

Sage

"Sage, they're here!" Abby calls down to me.

I finish pulling my hair back and get ready to meet the couple who wants to buy the B&B.

After I got about four hours of sleep yesterday, we met with the lawyer and found out her parents had put Abby's name on everything, so there is no probate period. The business, checking account, the land deeds, all of it have her name, which means she can sell the B&B right away.

Since there is no one else listed on the will and no family members, we're free to move forward with everything. After we left the attorney's office, we went to the funeral home. That's where it seemed to hit Abby.

Sadly, none of the funeral arrangements had been planned, but there was enough money in her parents' account to cover everything. She did well picking out coffins, gravesites, and headstones, and setting up the funeral arrangements. The funeral home was amazing in helping with all the details. They are handling pretty much everything.

We came home and planned to have the wake here at the B&B, so we discussed the food and drinks. The caterer the B&B uses for events agreed to come in and do the wake for half price, so we met with her this morning.

Abby wants to do all her Mom and Dad's favorite foods, and the caterer is on board, having known her parents for so long.

After the caterer, we run out to the store and get boxes and rent a truck so we can put things into storage until she figures out her next steps. She has been sorting through her parents' room.

Surprisingly, sorting through her parents' things has been easy for her, almost comforting. Thank goodness for small blessings. I suggest we just pack everything up so she can go through it later when she's ready, but she wants to do it now.

I've been texting with Colt nonstop about all the details. We talk a few times a day and had video chatted last night, but it's still hard being away. I miss him like crazy. I miss him more than when I left town seven years ago. I can't wait to get home to him. It's looking like another week still, and we don't have a solid date.

I swipe on some lip gloss and head out to meet the couple.

"Sage! This is Adam and Lauren Willis. They want to buy the B&B!"

I go to shake hands, but Lauren wraps me in a tight hug followed by Adam.

"Grace and Abby have gushed about you and told us so much. We're so glad to meet you!" Lauren says. She's bubbly and so full of energy. I think she will do great at the B&B here.

"Let's sit on the front porch. I have some tea and cookies. I'll go grab them," Abby says.

"Oh, let me help you!" Lauren insists.

I lead Adam out to the sitting area on the front porch that has a wicker couch and two wicker chairs. I let him take the couch, and I take a chair.

I watch him take in the front porch and yard.

"Abby tells me you two had your honeymoon here?"

He smiles. "Yes, eleven years ago now. We've been back once or twice a year ever since. We love it. About three years ago, we talked to

Grace and Stan. When and if they were ever interested in selling it, we'd be interested in buying it. Last year, they started talking about retiring and knew Abby didn't want the place. We did a lot of talking and had some appraisals done all via their lawyer. If the numbers are where they were last year, we have a price ready. If things have changed too much, we'll need a day to go over everything."

"I understand. I haven't seen anything with the business end. I'm here for whatever Abby needs. I know she wants a fast sale. She's coming home to Texas with me for a bit while she gets started on school."

"Well, we can pay cash if the price is what we talked to her parents about. We've been saving for this place for a while. It's been our dream."

"Oh, you started business talk without us," Lauren says as she comes out holding a plate of oatmeal cookies. Abby follows behind her with a pitcher of sweet tea and some glasses.

Lauren sits next to her husband on the couch, and I can't help but think they make such a cute couple. They're going to fit into this B&B for sure with their Southern accents and charm.

Lauren has her blond hair pulled to the side and curled with very natural-looking makeup, wearing a beautiful summer dress. Adam has dark hair, wearing nicely worn jeans and a button-down shirt. They gravitate toward each other. He pulls her close, and she goes almost without thinking.

I smile at Abby with her light-brown hair in a braid wearing her maxi dress. She's the perfect Southern belle she was raised to be. I love it here, and I think the place will flourish with Lauren and Adam.

"So, Adam was telling me if the price is what they talked to your parents about last year, they can pay cash and close pretty soon."

"I think everything should be close to the same. We've stayed well booked and had a few weddings. Mom and Dad did a few upgrades to the kitchen and one of the bathrooms. We have a meeting with the attorney tomorrow morning who handles all the business books. We'll know where we stand then."

"Are you sure you're ready to sell so soon?" Lauren asks.

"Yes, I never wanted to run this place. I want to be a midwife. I love you guys. You're meant to run this place, I feel it. You have the energy and love it as much as they did. I think this is what they would want."

Lauren dabs at her eyes like she's trying to stop a tear from falling.

"You know you're welcome anytime. Both of you, right?"

"Thanks." Abby smiles.

We sit on the porch and talk a bit about some of the events the B&B has hosted and what Grace has done for holidays and such.

When a black van pulls up to the curb, Abby stiffens.

"Who is that?" I ask.

"The church," she says.

I smile at Lauren and Adam. "Why don't you guys walk the house and the grounds. Get a feel for it? We have to talk to this gentleman."

"Of course! We'll see you for dinner, right?"

"Yes, we'll be there."

Adam and Lauren walk inside as three men walk up the steps, heading towards us.

We stand to greet them.

"Hello, Abby," the taller one says. He has the air about him as being the leader, but something about his voice sends chills down my spine, and not the good ones.

"Hello, Pastor Luke. May I introduce my good friend Sage? Sage, this is Pastor Luke,

Assistant Pastor Mike, and this is Robby, the pastor's son."

"Nice to meet you all," I say and put on a fake smile. "Would you like to sit?"

They make their way to the couch and settle in.

They talk a bit, exchanging condolences. I see the name of the church on the van door and send it to Colt quickly. He had asked me about it the night before.

"Everything okay, Sage?" Luke asks.

"Oh yes, sorry. My family has been checking in with me several times a day. There are a lot of us and being so close, someone is always checking in on me. They worry if I don't answer." I smile at him sweetly.

"It's nice to have such a big support system," he replies.

"It is." I limit my responses. I want them to talk. A trick Dad taught me. You let people talk themselves into a hole while you smile and listen.

"Well, we have a few matters of business we came to talk about."

"Figured you did. Let's get on with it," I say.

"These are private matters between Abby and the church," Luke says.

"Sage is staying," she says.

He eyes me, and I get a very uneasy feeling from him.

"From what I understand, Abby has no interest in your church, so I'm not sure what business you could possibly have with her," I say.

His eyes narrow. Yeah, they don't like strong women one bit. This is going to be fun. I send Colt a quick text telling him I'm going to call him so he can hear this but to be quiet. I place the call and set the phone in my lap.

Call it gut instinct, but I have a feeling something isn't right.

"Well, first, there's the matter of your parents' estate. As you may know, when a church member dies, they are required to leave twenty-five percent of their estate to the church. I was informed your parents didn't do that. So, we need to rectify that as soon as possible."

Are these people fucking kidding?

"You can't be serious," I say.

"We most certainly are," Luke replies. The other two men have yet to speak a word.

"Well, good luck enforcing that. You're right. Her parents left you nothing, and that's what you'll get. Everything was left to Abby."

I watch his face go red. “Well, that leads us into the next matter. It isn’t proper for a lady to own such a high-income business per the church regulations. You’ll need to get married, so we’ve set up a marriage for you and Robby here.”

I watch Abby’s face go pale. I take a deep breath before I lose my shit.

“Excuse me?! This is the twenty-first century, and she very well can own anything she likes. It’s also against the law to force a woman to marry someone she chooses not to. And let me repeat my earlier statement, Abby has no interest in your church. So, you have no control over her. Now, we’re going to kindly ask you to leave,” I say and stand, taking my phone in my hand.

Pastor Luke looks more than pissed off, but I’m sure knowing we’re on a public street, he needs to watch what is said.

“This isn’t over,” Luke says to Abby.

“Yes, it is. Anything more you have to say can be done through her lawyer who I will have get in touch with you right away. If you continue to contact and harass Abby, she’ll file harassment charges. The recording of today’s conversation will be attached to the police report." I hold the phone and watch Robby's face pale.

With that, I walk over to Abby and place my arm around her waist and lead her inside, leaving the three men on the porch.

"Hold it together. Let's get to your room," I tell her.

When we get there, she sits on the bed and cries.

I put the phone to my ear.

"Colt, you hear all that?"

"Yes," he bites out.

"I'm going to call the lawyer and let him know what's going on."

"I'm going to call a local private investigator up there. I'll have him do some digging. If they're forcing arranged marriages, I'm guessing the church isn't all squeaky clean."

"Okay, have them dig fast."

"I will. Stay safe and keep your gun on you."

"I promise. I love you."

"Love you too, Sage."

We hang up, and I wrap my arms around Abby. We lie in bed, and she finally lets it all out.

Chapter 19

Sage

I look around the funeral home, and tensions are high. It's been a few days since the church members showed up at the B&B and today, we burry Abby's parents. Many members of the church come, and all sit on one side while friends and people supporting Abby sit on the other.

Lauren and Adam have been right by our side with everything and have taken so much pressure off Abby. I'm so grateful. The service is about to start when a man in a suit sits next to me.

When I look up, I see Colt, and my jaw drops. He rests his forehead on mine.

"I know this isn't a happy event, but you still look sexy as hell," he whispers.

"I can't believe you're here," I say with tears in my eyes.

"We were all talking at dinner the other night. We all wanted to come but knew we couldn't, so I said I would. I have to head back tomorrow night. We're short on ranch hands, but I couldn't let you do this alone."

I wrap my hand around his neck. "You're the most amazing man, Colton Evans Buchanan, and I love you with everything I am."

I watch his eyes mist over and fill with love. "I'm head over heels in love with you, Sage Ella-Rose Buchanan, and I'm going to spend the rest of my life proving it to you."

He places a soft kiss on my lips, and I feel a hand on my arm.

"Sage, who is this?" Abby whispers, and I laugh.

I look at Colt one more time then take his hand in mine and turn to Abby.

"This is Colt. Colt, this is Abby, Lauren, and Adam," I introduce him, and they say a quick hello before the funeral director starts.

On the way to the gravesite, Adam and Lauren drive us all there. Colt doesn't let go of my hand once. After the service is over, I point out the members of the church to Colt, and he nods.

"I have some paperwork you need to see when we get to the B&B," he whispers in my ear. I nod and take Abby's hand in mine and walk over to Pastor Luke and his family.

"Anything you have to say to Abby, Lauren, or Adam should be done here, as I think it's best you don't attend the wake. It's at the B&B, and you aren't welcome," I say in a firm, cold voice.

Luke stands a bit straighter. "So be it. I'd like to have a meeting with Abby sooner rather than later."

Colt speaks up. "Fine. Tomorrow morning at nine a.m. at the bakery up the road from the B&B. We'll be there."

He then puts one arm around Abby's waist and takes my hand and leads us to the car.

Lauren and Adam follow us in. Once we're pulling out of the graveyard, Colt speaks.

"I was going to wait, but I need you guys to be informed. This can't leave this car, understand?" We all agree.

"I put a private investigator not only on the church but on that Luke guy. Something about leaving twenty-five percent when church members die and the forced marriage rubbed me the wrong way, and my instinct was correct."

Adam looks at Colt in the review mirror, and Lauren turns from the front passenger seat to face him. Abby's spine goes straight.

"There were four church deaths last year. One of them was confirmed to have left the money to the church, which would have been over a half million dollars, yet the church only claimed half that all year long. So, where did the money go?"

"Always follow the money," I say.

Colt gives a halfhearted smile. "Always follow the money. Luke bought a new house in cash that's worth, take a wild guess."

"Half a million dollars?" Lauren says.

"Exactly. There are also two cases where he forced his older two sons into marriages to take over the assets of the woman for the church. He takes the money but leaves everything in the woman's name, so it all falls back on her when something goes wrong. Those women shockingly haven't been seen in public for a while. My private investigator thought the amount of security around Luke's home was unnecessary for a pastor. Via some not very legal methods, he did some digging and found those women and several others being held in his basement. I'll spare you the details, but let's say it was enough to make my stomach turn."

"I can't meet with them tomorrow," Abby whispers.

"You aren't going alone. Sage and I will be there. We need him to confirm his plans with you, your business, etc. while I'm wearing a wire. I've already been in contact with the authorities, and it was pushed up to the FBI. I guess they've been watching him, and this is the break they need to go after him. They plan to raid everything at once, so there's no time to hide anything. The church, his house, along with the homes of several of the church leaders. So, we have to go in like nothing is wrong. If you don't talk, so be it."

"Will it be safe?" Adam asks.

"Yes, there are several undercover agents around today and will be at the wake and in the coffee shop tomorrow. For added protection, one of the guests at the B&B tonight will also be an undercover cop, but I don't know which one. Again, not a word can be spoken of this once we open the car doors. There are ears everywhere, and we can't trust anyone."

Everyone nods. Then Abby looks up at Lauren.

“If you guys want to run the other way and forget the B&B I completely understand.”

They both laugh. “We don’t scare easily. If you knew my childhood, you would understand,” Lauren murmurs. This is when I get a good look at her.

“You might have more in common with Colt and me than you realize,” I say, and we lock eyes. She nods as we pull into the driveway.

“Remember, not a word. Not even tonight behind closed doors, okay? No texting, nothing. Act like you don’t know; we can’t risk it.” We all nod at Colt and head into the wake.

•••••••••••

I hate wakes. It feels like it never ends. People linger and want us to comfort them, and I just don’t have it in me. Finally, Adam and Lauren take over and push people out with excuses that Abby needs to be alone.

Even once the place is cleared, none of us are willing to sleep. The guests stay up with us, and I know we’re all watching them, trying to figure out who is the undercover cop.

Is it the middle-aged business couple here on vacation from New York City? Maybe it’s the woman and her fiancé here checking out wedding venues in town. I rule out the little old lady who is making her pilgrimage to Graceland. She's in her eighties. I thought for a moment maybe it's even Adam and Lauren.

But my bet is the on the gentleman in his early thirties who's in town for a family reunion. He says he wants to have a place of peace to come to escape his crazy family.

No matter who it is, my gun is always on me. Colt knows it too. He has made sure of it and has never left my side. I never leave Abby's side, so the three of us share her room. Thankfully, Colt and I can squeeze into my bed. With Abby in her bed on the other side of the room, I can tell isn't sleeping, but she has told us several times, she is happy to have Colt in the room.

We're now getting ready for our coffee meeting, and tensions are high. Adam and Lauren stay at the B&B to handle checkouts and the guests. They've taken to the place, learning the ropes quickly.

Colt will drive us and promises not to leave our side. The car ride to the coffee shop is quiet, and I know Abby is terrified. Sadly, Colt and I have both been in worse situations. That doesn't mean we aren't nervous either. It's the fear of the unknown.

Colt parks the car and we take a deep breath as he checks his phone.

"Okay, let's do this," he says. He guides us both into the coffee shop. We don't see Luke, Mike, or Robby there yet, so we get in line to get a coffee. Then we take a seat by the front window, out in the open.

We only wait about five minutes before Luke and Mike show up, but no Robby. They don't even bother getting coffee. They just sit at our table, with their backs to the front door. Abby won't make eye contact with them, which is for the best.

You can tell by the way Luke carries himself, he's over-confident, and I know this will be his downfall. As he sits, he unbuttons his suit coat and looks over at Abby.

"Let's get right down to business, shall we?" Luke asks in an irritated tone.

I must bite the inside of my cheek not to smile. I feel Colt's hand dig into my thigh as a reminder as well. He knows me all too well.

"Go on," Colt says.

"Abigale, your parents were registered members of the church. They had signed that they acknowledged the rule upon becoming members."

"When was this?" Colt interrupts.

"The date we have on file was right after they were married in 1988."

"So, thirty-two years ago." I do the math.

"Regardless, they knew the rules. Their estate has to pay out the twenty-five percent," Luke states.

"Just to clarify. Twenty-five percent of what?" Colt asks.

"Of their net worth," Mike speaks up for the first time.

"And what about your demands on Abby if she wants to keep the bed and breakfast?"

"Women cannot own such a high-profile, high-income business. She has no choice but to marry Robby to continue to own such a company."

At this, I sit up straight, and Colt again knows what's coming. I want to reach across the table and rip off this guy's balls and force-feed them to him. But Colt remains calm and grips my thigh even tighter.

It's a reminder that not only calms me but turns me on too.

"Okay, let's play your little game. She marries Robby. Then what happens to the business?" Colt asks.

"Well, Robby and the church would run it for her, of course," Luke says like we should already know that.

"But it stays in her name?" Colt asks.

"Of course," Mike says. Colt nods.

"And if she doesn't agree to marry Robby?"

"Then we will take her to court for the twenty-five percent of the estate, which will include twenty-five percent of the value of the bed and breakfast."

Bingo.

"So. let me get this straight," I say. I rub Colt's arm to let him know I'm calm and in control.

"If she doesn't marry Robby, you will go after her for twenty-five percent. But if she does, then you forget the twenty-five percent, but the church then runs the bed and breakfast?"

"Yes," Luke says. I smile, which seems to confuse him.

"Why would she pick either option? This is America, and she's free to do what she wants. Women have equal rights, and your case would be laughed out of any courtroom. Plus, I'm sure you wouldn't want to bring the eye of the state or the government on your business dealings, now would you?" Colt states.

I love watching Luke squirm more than I should. He knows we have more on him than he thought. That over-confidence he had moments ago is gone.

Before he can respond, I hear the ding that states someone has walked into the shop. I look at the door over Luke's shoulder and smile. Showtime.

"But it's too late," Colt starts. "Because the state and the FBI have been looking into you for longer than you realize, and you just admitted to this plan. That's illegal, and you just gave them what they need. While we've been sitting here chatting, the FBI has been raiding not only your home, but Mike's home, the church, and the home of several of your higher-ups. I know what they've found in your basement." Watching Luke's face pale puts a smile on my face.

Right then, four uniformed officers come behind Luke and Mike and whip their arms into handcuffs before they have time to react. The cops read them their Miranda rights and take them out to the waiting cars.

A man in a suit walks up to Colt and shakes his hand. "Thank you for everything, Colt."

"Well, I'd do anything for my girl here, and she would do anything for the people closest to her. It was a no brainer," Colt says as he removes the wire he's been wearing.

"Hello ladies, I'm Detective Ryan Green, FBI. I need to get your statements on the case. I'd prefer you come down to the station, but we can also do it at the bed and breakfast if that's more comfortable."

I look at Abby. "It's up to you. I'm where you are."

She nods and smiles. "I can go down to the station."

On shaky legs, we head to the car and prepare for what will be several hours of questions, I'm sure. But having Colt here? I won't care if it's several days of questions.

Chapter 20

Colt

We end up spending four hours at the police station. The lawyer I've been working with meets us there. He will represent Abby. They have the most questions for Abby since she has been going to the church for years, as her parents have asked.

The charges that come from the raids on the homes of the church officials pile up. They currently have enough to charge them on kidnapping, tax evasion, blackmail, human rights abuse, physical abuse, and several theft crimes.

Many of the church elders also have unregistered weapons and domestic abuse charges upon raiding their homes. A few have some drug charges pile up as well. All are hit with tax evasion charges too.

To say it's a mess is an understatement. Due to the questions and a few things needed for the bed and breakfast to be sold, I have to leave Sage in Memphis. She will be a bit longer.

That was a week ago. I miss her like crazy, and I think my brothers see me becoming a bit unhinged. Talking and texting Sage every day and nightly video calls aren't enough anymore. I need my girl back in my arms.

I need to hold her, touch her, kiss her. It's not even about sex. I just need that physical touch to reconnect. I need to know she's coming home and above all, I need to make her mine.

The phone sex in our nightly video call the other night was freakin hot as hell. She had been in the bathtub when I called. Seeing her so relaxed, surrounded by bubbles and the water running down her tan skin, is an image that still makes me hard.

I need to get my ring on her and get her down the aisle. Now that I have set the idea in my head, every day her ring finger is bare kills me. We've had so much hold us apart so far, I'm just ready to start my life with her. I want the life we've been planning—the kids, the growing old together, the family vacations, all of it.

I've waited seven years just to get her back. One would think I could be patient for another few weeks. Wrong. Every day stretches out and feels like years. Like my life and my heart are just on pause because she isn't here.

"Hey man, I need some help at the bar tonight," Jason says and pats me on the back.

I'm pretty sure he doesn't need the help. This is just his way of distracting me, but I'm going to take it.

Sage is supposed to be home the day after tomorrow, but things have come up twice already, moving the date back. I don't have too much hope she'll make it home then.

"Yeah, I'll be there. What time?"

"Does five work? I need some prep help before we get too busy tonight."

Being it's a Saturday night, the whole town will be out. On Friday and Saturday nights, Jason brings in live music and has a few food specials, making it the place to be. Those two nights make his income for the week easily.

"That works."

He pats me on the shoulder and walks off again. I check my phone again. Nothing from Sage. Now I have four hours before I need to be at the bar. I send Sage a quick text letting her know I'm helping Jason out tonight. Then I try to focus on some of the bookwork in front of me.

Once I find my groove, the bookwork keeps me busy. We're prepping for the final cow sale before winter, and I have made some good headway in the paperwork.

I head up to the main house and just stand in the doorway of Sage's room, our room. I love this room, but it feels so empty without her, even though she's all over the room. I notice a new photo on the dresser I don't remember being there. Sage and I are sitting on the back of my truck on our ice cream date. I remember Sage taking the picture of us, but I don't remember seeing it on the dresser before. I guess she put it up before she left.

I look over the other photos on the dresser. She and I at senior prom. She and Blaze at the Grand Canyon. All of us standing in front of this house the day we moved in. One of her and Abby with whom I assume are Abby's parents. There are a few scattered ones of people I don't know. With Sage being so young in the photos, I guess they're from her travels.

The last picture catches my eye. I'm leaning up against the metal gate one day while the guys and I were working cattle. I have on my old pair of leather chaps. I've replaced those over a year ago, so this photo is at least a year old. I'm not looking at the camera so that would be why I don't remember her taking the picture. Trucks and farm vehicles are in the background, but they're blurred. The cows are in front, but they're blurred too. It's completely focused on me, showing that the photo was intentional.

I take a deep breath at the thought. She took that photo of me and had it set up here in her room all this time. Even the photo of her and I at prom has been on the dresser for a while. If there is ever a doubt in anything she has told me, this wipes it away. I have photos of Sage on my phone and one in my wallet because I just couldn't let her go either.

With one last glance at the photos, I head in to take a shower and get dressed. I decide to return Sage's favor from the other morning. She sent me a picture of her outfit for the day. This isn't something I normally do, but the thought of her drooling over my photo like I did hers has its appeal.

I send her the picture with a short text.

Me: Heading out to the bar for the night. I'll have my phone on me. Call anytime.

Before I can put my phone away, I see the three little dots showing she's typing. I didn't know until that moment how much I need that.

Sage: Damn. I do have the sexiest boyfriend. How did I get so lucky?

Me: I am the one who got lucky that you fell in love with me. But I miss you like hell.

Sage: I miss you too. Will you call me when you get home from the bar tonight? I don't care what time.

Me: Of course I will. Still looking like the day after tomorrow you'll be home?

Sage: Yep. I'm not letting anything stop me this time.

Me: Good. I'm stealing you away to our cabin that night, just you and me.

Sage: I can't wait. I have to go, but I'll be waiting for your call tonight.

Me: Talk to you tonight. Be safe.

I can feel the smile on my face, thankful for the distraction of the bar tonight.

Soon as I walk into the bar, Jason has things for me to do from helping him prep the bar to helping the band set up. He has me tend bar a bit, claiming some paperwork that is overdue. He even has me waiting on a few tables.

I welcome the distraction. After the dinner rush, I sit at a table and listen to the band. They're a local band and are pretty good. Brice and his dad walk in and stop to say hi to me.

I want to hate Brice because he dated Sage a few months back, but knowing Sage dated him only because she was lonely, makes it feel like it's more my fault than anything. If I hadn't been making up excuses, she wouldn't have felt lonely and wouldn't have gone out with him.

It's not his fault, and I know what it's like to have Sage and then lose her. I feel a bit bad for him. I'm also thankful for him intervening with Kelli at the café. For this reason alone, I'm nice and hold a conversation. They end up sitting at the table next to me, and we chat a bit between songs.

I'm talking to Brice's dad about winter prep work we have coming up when I hear a voice that now sounds like nails on a chalkboard.

"Colt! Haven't seen you here in a while." Kelli says, and she promptly sits on my lap.

What.

The.

Fuck.

I would never put my hand on a woman in anger, but anger is all I feel right now. I have very few options to get her off me.

"Kelli, get the fuck off me now."

She laughs. "Too late, the damage is done." She looks toward the door. I see Sage and Abby. The look of absolute hurt and rage in Sage's eyes tells me I just hurt my girl. Again.

I stand, dumping Kelli on the floor. I intend to go after Sage, but she and Abby are out the door before I can even get Kelli off my feet. That's when it clicks into place. This has been a calculated move on Kelli's part.

Doing something I swore I'd never do, I raise my voice to a lady. Though Kelli is the furthest thing from a lady.

"What the fuck is wrong with you!" I bellow so loud, the whole bar quiets down.

Kelli tries to get up as gracefully as possible, which resembles a baby calf learning how to walk.

"I did you a favor, Colt," she coos as she tries to put her hand on my chest. "We both know we're meant to be together."

"No, Kelli," I say, taking a step back. "I've been in love with Sage since I was thirteen; it's always been her. I fucked things up, and you were just a distraction. You're the one who lied and connived to keep us apart for years now. But we see you for the snake you are. Don't you ever come near me, Sage, or our family again. So help me God, I will air all your dirty laundry for the town to see."

I am fuming at this point, so when Kelli bursts into tears and runs off, I don't even care. I try to calm down when I feel a hand on my shoulder. I swing around, ready to take a swing at whoever it is, male or female. I find Jason blocking my arm.

"Hey man, deep breath. You need to calm down and go after Sage. We all know what she's thinking right now, and you know we'll back your story, but you need to fix this now. Tonight. Do not wait."

I look around and see Brice and his dad nodding in agreement with Jason. I rub my hand down my face. "Fuck!"

I pat Jason on the shoulder and head out to my truck. If she showed up early with Abby in tow, my guess is her next stop is the house to get Abby settled. That's where I'm heading too.

Chapter 21

Sage

I'm so excited to surprise Colt. I want to tell him we're coming home early, but I know the surprise will be so much better. So, for that reason, I haven't been texting or talking to him much today. I don't want to let the surprise slip.

This is also the reason I've insisted on driving most of the way. If I'm driving, I can't be on my phone, so it makes it all a bit easier.

Then the picture of him before he heads to the bar comes in, and oh my word, it is so hard not to drool. I miss him something fierce, and that's why Abby and I bust our butts to head home a few days early.

I haven't even told any of the family I'm coming home early. I don't want the surprise to get out. I do call Mom and ask her to set up one of the guest rooms for me, so she went over earlier today and made sure it was cleaned and has fresh towels and sheets.

We stop on the other side of Dallas for a bathroom break and to grab something to eat. Once back in the car, I run my idea past Abby.

"How would you feel about stopping by the bar and surprising Colt? You can meet Jason too. We have to pass the bar on the way to the ranch anyway."

Abby smiles. "I love the idea. I can't wait to see this place. You've talked about it so much."

Abby bounces out of her seat the closer we get. I can tell how excited she is. This is a new start for her, one where she can decide her future and the path she takes. I'm so excited for her and so relieved to be out of Memphis. A place that felt like home for so long no longer has that safe feel to it.

As we near Rock Springs, we see the neon lights of the bar and all the cars in the parking lot. It really is the place to be tonight. Abby asks questions about the town and the bar as we park and get out of the car.

I can't take my eyes off Abby. I love seeing her experience a place like this for the first time. She's just so bubbly and full of excitement.

I open the door, and the music from the live band gets louder. My eyes scan the room for Colt, but when I see him, my blood runs cold. What I see is Kelli sitting on his lap, laughing.

Abby must see him a second later. I hear, "Oh, Sugar," in my ear.

Colt sees me, and he stands so fast, Kelli falls on her ass on the dirty bar floor. While it's a little bit satisfying, that's erased away when I see his face shows the telltale signs of guilt. It's all my heart can take. I don't see anyone else. I don't hear anything but my heart pounding in my ears.

I grab Abby's hand, turn around, and head right back out the door to my truck. We climb in, and I head toward the ranch. I have to get Abby situated.

In the corner of my eye, I see Abby open her mouth to speak. "Just, I can't right now," I say to stop her, and she closes her mouth.

Trying to figure out my next steps, I turn on the radio. After a few songs, I pull out my phone and call Megan who I know is home.

"Megan, don't ask questions. Just meet me outside. I'm going to be at the ranch in about fifteen minutes. I need you to take Abby and her bags to her room. Don't ask any questions. I can't do it right now. Abby can tell you all about it."

"Okay, Sage. I'm sitting on the steps now waiting. I'll be here."

"Thank you."

I hang up, and Abby looks at me.

"You aren't staying?" she asks.

"The house is where Colt will look for me. I need some time to think. Megan will get you all settled, and I'll be back for breakfast."

"Okay, I'm here if you need me."

I smile as much as I can, which isn't much at all. As I pull into the driveaway, I can't even enjoy how Abby's eyes grow wide over the tree-lined driveway that gives way to the massive two-story house.

Like she promised, Megan is sitting on the porch steps by the kitchen door. I park the car and make sure Abby is handed off safely to Megan.

"I got her. I'm going to bribe the story out of her with some chocolate cake. Take care of you."

I hug her. "I'll be back for breakfast. Just need some space."

I head to the barn and grab the keys for the four-wheeler and rev it up. I take it to the back of the property to the one place I can always think. The quiet night and the rev of the motor provide just enough white noise.

I replay the scene at the bar back in my head over and over. Was waiting an extra week for me too much? I never pegged Colt for that type of guy. And right in Jason's bar! Where the hell was Jason? If he had seen Colt, I know he'd have punched him in the face and thrown him out on his ass so fast.

Has Colt kept Kelli on the side this whole time? Why put so much effort into winning me back and gaining my trust? Why come out to Memphis and put the effort in with the private investigator.

So many questions I won't get the answers to tonight. I need time to decompress from all this. Tomorrow, I'll have a conversation that doesn't involve me punching Colt in the face.

The cabin that has always been my safe place comes into view, and my heart feels lighter already. I park the four-wheeler behind the cabin and head inside. I don't even bother to flip on the lights. I take off my boots, crawl into bed, and let the tears fall.

•••••••••••

At some point, I drift off to sleep, but I awake to the sound of the old wooden door closing. The living room light is turned on, letting light flow into the bedroom. Being only one person knows this is the cabin I'd be at, I don't even have to turn around to know who it is.

A quick glance at the clock tells me I've been here for about an hour. I just want to go back to sleep and deal with all this tomorrow.

"Go away," I mumble, knowing he won't listen anyway.

"It's not what it looked like." Colt's deep timbre comes from the doorway and even though I'm mad and hurt, the sound of his voice still does something to my body. Still makes me crave him.

"It never is."

"Come on. Jason was right there behind the bar. You think I'm that stupid, or that he'd let me out of the building alive?"

I don't answer him, and he doesn't need me to as he continues talking, "She walked in and sat down on my lap not thirty seconds before I saw you. She had just gotten there. I hadn't seen her all night. I was told as I left, she had walked in and made a beeline to me."

"How convenient," I mutter again, still not bothering to look at him. It's one thing to hear his voice, but a whole other thing to look into his sexy as sin eyes.

"I was telling her to get off, trying so hard not to put my hands on her to remove her. I was so pissed, Sage. You of all people know I will never touch a woman in anger, no matter how much they deserve it. I'm not my father."

I know this about Colt. We've had many conversations about this. He was always worried about turning into his father, but he's such a better person than that. Even this little bit tonight proves it. I know that in the back of my mind, even if my heart won't believe it right now.

I still don't say anything, but I hear him take a step toward the bed.

"What you didn't see was her laughing and saying she knew you were coming, and she did me a favor. Saying we belonged together. You didn't see me yelling at her so loud, every single person in the bar looked. You didn't see her running off in tears because of how bad I humiliated her."

I hear him take his boots off and feel the other side of the bed dip down. He doesn't make a move to crawl in closer to me. He just stays on the other side of the bed.

"Call Jason and ask him. He was right there behind the bar and saw it all. Brice and his dad were at the table next to me. Call them. I had been talking with them on and off all night."

I finally take a deep breath and roll over to look at him. His voice had betrayed him. Though his voice sounds steady and sure, the pain in his face is clear as day. He looks at me and when he sees my tears, his eyes water as well.

"I was so excited to surprise you. I didn't see Kelli in the parking lot. I was talking to Abby. She had so many questions about the bar and the town. Walking in and seeing that, it was like a knife to the heart. Worse than when I came home for Megan's graduation."

Silent tears run down his face now as he watches me and listens. I reach up and carefully wipe away the tears running down his face. He holds my hand to his face and closes his eyes. He soaks up any comfort I give him.

I know in my heart he's telling the truth, but my mind is now telling me to be more guarded. I lean in and lightly kiss him. He gives me control of the kiss, and I keep it light before pulling back.

"I'm still calling Brice to confirm your story," I whisper.

He nods. "I know."

I sigh and sit up on the edge of the bed.

"Kelli needs to watch her back. I will be getting revenge, and don't you dare try to talk me out of it," I say and look over my shoulder. He just nods. I head over to the cabin phone to call Brice.

His story is spot on to Colt's, but he shares what Colt said to her and how people were talking after Colt left. I guess no one feels sorry for Kelli, and everyone is rooting for us.

After I hang up with Brice, I call Jason. He relays the same story and then begs me not to hold Colt responsible for this. Kelli has had it out to try to break us up for years. I know this but hearing someone else say it is like a slap in the face reminder.

I return to the bed and lie on my side of the bed. Colt lies on his back, staring at the ceiling. He rolls his head to the side and watches me.

"Ever get the feeling the whole universe is working against us?" I ask.

"That thought has crossed my mind a time or two," he whispers and turns to his side to face me. "But I'd walk through hell and fire and ten thousand spiders to get to you."

I smile and lean in and kiss him gently. This time, he takes control of the kiss. He flips me onto my back and is over me in an instant, never breaking the kiss.

"For the record, the thought of another woman touching me makes me want to claw my own skin off. I'm yours. Only yours," he says before sitting up and pulling off his shirt.

In the next instant, he has my shirt off. The hunger in his eyes must match mine. I watch his eyes run down my whole body before his control snaps.

"Clothes off now," he growls at me, and we're in a race to see who can shed their clothes the fastest.

Once naked, he grabs my ankles and pulls me, so my ass is on the edge of the bed. He hits his knees and pulls my thighs wide.

Before my mind can catch up, I feel his mouth on my clit. All sane thought leaves my head. Colt learned long ago how to play my body like a fine instrument, and it's like riding a bike. He's right back at being a master.

With just a few short licks and swirls of his tongue on my clit, I'm already on edge. I reach down and grab his hair, holding his head in place. If he stops, I think I might truly die.

All I can do is moan his name over and over again.

"I've got you, baby," he says as he glides two fingers inside me and thrusts them in and out lazily, driving me insane and keeping me right on the edge.

I thrust my hips up, looking for just a little something more. Colt hums while licking my clit. He hooks his fingers, rubbing that magical spot inside me, and I shatter, screaming his name and locking my thighs around his head.

When I finally relax, I don't think I can move to save my life. I watch Colt sit up and bring his fingers that were just inside me to his mouth and lick them clean.

He kisses my clit one more time, causing my hips to jerk since they are still so sensitive. He kisses his way up to my belly button and further up to my breasts. He takes one nipple into his mouth and circles his tongue around it, then he does the other.

He then kisses his way up to my neck and runs his teeth over my pulse point there and then sucks my earlobe into his mouth. By the time he makes it to my jaw, I'm already going crazy for him again.

He takes my mouth in a sweet, soft kiss and lies beside me, and turns me on my side, so he's spooning me from behind with my head resting on his bicep.

Without a word, he pulls my leg backward over his hips and angles his hips, so the head of his cock is at my entrance but doesn't thrust in. I feel his warm breath on my ear.

"I love you, Sage. I am going to prove it to you tonight, so you never doubt me again."

"I love you too, Colt," I say on a moan as he slides into me to the hilt with a slow thrusting pace.

He keeps his pace, slow and steady while he whispers how much he loves me in my ear. He moves his hand from my hip down to my clit and makes lazy circles there. His other hand reaches around and tugs on my nipples, rubbing them between his fingers.

He picks up the pace only slightly when he leans down and runs my earlobe between his teeth, causing me to arch my back. His speed increases even more, and he presses on my clit even harder.

"Come for me now, Sage. I need to feel your pussy squeezing my cock. Dammit, come now!" He roars, and I do. My whole body locks up as the most intense climax of my life hits me.

I hear Colt moan my name somewhere in the distance as I struggle to take my next breath. When I come down from the most amazing high, I feel him still lazily thrusting in and out of me to prolong my orgasm.

"Wow."

"Yeah, wow! We need a shower," he says with a sexy smirk on his face.

Chapter 22

Colt

I wake to the sun filling the room in the cabin. Sage is wrapped around me like a spider monkey, her head on my shoulder, her arm across my chest, and her leg draped over my hips. This is how I want to wake up every day for the rest of my life.

I look at Sage still asleep, and I smile. I wore her out last night. After we made love in the shower, we stumbled into the kitchen for a snack and fed each other before I had her again on the kitchen table. By the time we made it back to bed, we were both tired. Somehow, I still ended up waking her up twice because I kept waking up needing her.

I lightly run my hand up and down her naked back, thinking about being inside her last night. Now, I'm hard as steel, but I know my girl needs a break. She stirs and before she even opens her eyes, a smile graces her face, and she kisses my neck.

I groan. "Baby, I know your sore. You need to stop." I feel her smile against my neck as she keeps kissing me.

She sits up, straddling my hips. Before I can think better, she's sliding down my cock. I grip her hips and groan. Nothing has ever felt so good. Nothing.

"God, baby, every time with you is better than the last. How is that possible?" I groan.

She groans and rides me faster. I grip her hips tighter and move her up and down my cock. Within moments, I feel her pussy clenching me, a sign she's close.

I sit up, pulling her tight against me as she keeps thrusting while I take her mouth. It causes enough friction on her clit for her orgasm to crash into her. She throws her head back and screams out my name. I kiss her neck, her collarbone, her shoulder as I thrust a few more times into her before I come, hard.

I come so hard for so long, you would never know I just had my girl multiple times the night before. I come so hard I see stars.

When we both come down, she's lying on top of me. My cock still buried in her is my new favorite place. We're both breathing hard.

We stay like that for a while before we get up and shower again and get dressed. We head back to the main house and walk in hand in hand, and everyone gives a sigh of relief. There's no one more relieved than me.

Sage lets go of my hand and walks over to Abby to hug her.

"Guys, this is Abby. She's going to be staying here as she figures out the next step in her life," Sage says.

Mom walks over to her. "I'm so sorry to hear about your parents. They took care of our Sage for us, and we'll now return the favor. Anything you need, you let us know. And you can call me Helen." She hugs her.

Everyone filters over and introduces themselves before we sit for breakfast.

"Okay, explain yourself. What happened?" Megan says once we sit.

I look over to Sage and take her hand. I nod at her, letting her know she can tell them as much or as little as she wants.

I watch her sigh. "Kelli is what happened. I saw, and I didn't get the full story, and I did what I do best. I ran."

I squeeze her hand. "If I had walked in on that, I'd have turned around and left too. I don't blame you one bit, but talking through it, last night? Just shows how far we've come."

She looks at me and smiles. She then tells the whole story over breakfast. Jason fills everyone in on the details from after Sage and Abby left.

"Well, I hope that bitch doesn't ever try to come into the beauty shop. I'll shave her bald," Megan says, and I watch jaws around the table fall open. "What?"

I smile. "Just never heard you talk that way." I smile again when she rolls her eyes.

After breakfast, everyone heads out, and Sage and I head upstairs to get some new clothes. When we walk into our room, she stops dead in her tracks.

"What's wrong?" I ask.

"You moved your stuff in here?"

"Well, yeah. I wasn't in my room anymore. Didn't make sense to keep going back and forth."

She looks around the room. I've added a few photos to the ones on her dresser. One of all of us the day I was adopted, another of my mom and me at the fair right before she died. She walks into the closet and sees my clothes across from hers. The closet is so big, it's only half full.

Then she walks into the bathroom where my stuff is mixed with hers. I lean my shoulder on the door jamb and watch her take it all in. She walks back up to me. Before I have time to react, she wraps her arms around me and hugs me.

"It's perfect," she says, and I smile. I kiss the top of her head and hold her. Because she's right. It's perfect.

Chapter 23

Sage

I wake up and can't help but smile. This past week since Abby arrived has been amazing and exactly what I've always pictured my life with Colt to be. I love waking up with him every morning.

I roll over only to find Colt isn't in bed, but an envelope sits on his pillow with my name on it. I can't help but smile as I open it and look at his masculine but beautiful writing.

Sage,

I have loved you since the moment I saw you when we were six. I started to know what that felt like when we were thirteen, and I knew at sixteen, I'd never let you go.

I plan to make that promise come true. Take a walk down memory lane with me. Head to the location where I saw you for the first time.

Colt

I jump out of bed and dress quickly in a pair of cut-off shorts I know Colt loves and a white tank top. I slip on a peach, turquoise, and brown flannel shirt but leave it open and roll up the sleeves. I put on my boots, leave my hair down, add on a bit of mascara, and head out the door.

When I get to the kitchen, I see a blueberry muffin and a to-go cup of coffee on the counter. I know this is Colt's way of making sure I eat. So, I take five minutes to eat the muffin then bring the coffee with me.

I head into the barn but don't see him, so I head up to the loft.

A little confused, I see Blaze in the corner where I hid that day he found me, but he smiles and hugs me.

"I know I wasn't the happiest when you told me about you and Colt, but I want you to know it's because I've always protected you. I knew he caused you so much pain. I just kept thinking if I had known, I could have protected you from it all."

"I caused him just as much pain."

"I know, and I only want what's best for you. I've been watching you two, and it's like you aren't yourselves without each other. I'm on your side always if you need to talk or vent, but I'm so happy for you. For both of you."

He brings tears to my eyes as he hugs me again.

"I love you, Sage. I will still do anything for you. All you ever have to do is ask."

"I love you too, Blaze. The same goes for me. Just ask."

He hugs me a bit harder before he pulls away and hands me another envelope that looks just like the one on my pillow this morning.

Sage,

My adoption day is a blur, but what I do remember is sitting and talking to you and falling more and more in love with you by the minute.

I promise to always remind you how much in love with you I am.

Meet me at the spot we ran away to after dinner that day.

Colt

I smile and hop in my truck to drive to the far side of the ranch where the ranch church is, remembering when we snuck away after dinner and sat in the back pew of the church and just talked.

We talked about the shitty parents we had, about how amazing Mom and Dad are, the type of parents we wanted to be when we grow up. Every time I think back to that night, it's with the realization that it was the night we planned our futures together.

When we have kids when we grow up when we get out of school. Our lives have been entangled from then on.

I pull up to the church and don't see anyone outside. Hoping to find Colt inside, I head in. Sitting in the back pew is Megan. I laugh.

She hops up and hugs me. "I think this place holds memories for everyone in their own way. It draws us to it even when we don't realize it."

I smile. "It does." I look around the church. It's always been a place of comfort for me.

She hands me another envelope and watches as I read it.

Sage,

That night when we had to head back to the house, I remember a feeling of dread of not wanting to let you go. I didn't sleep at all that night, trying to figure out what that meant.

I know now what it means.

I love you.

I promise to spend my life making you feel that way too.

A few weeks later, we had our first kiss. Head to the spot where you turned my world upside down in the best possible way.

Colt

I can't help the tears that fall down my cheek.

"He's a good one, even with the bad boy reputation," Megan says with a smile on her face.

"Yes, he is," I agree and then rush back to my truck.

I follow the old driveway up past Mom and Dad's house to the family graveyard. I see Dad standing by the gate.

"Hey baby girl," he says and hugs me. "I have to know the story behind this stop," he says.

I laugh. "Not long after Colt was adopted, he found me out here standing at the gate. He asked what was on my mind. I said I was getting to know our new family. It was weird. I had heard stories from Blaze about many of the people in the graveyard but having them being my family felt weird."

I smile, remembering that day as I look out over the gravestones. "He took my hand, and we walked each row, reading each headstone and sharing the stories we knew. When we walked out, we stood under that tree." I point to the tree at the corner of the turn off to the graveyard. "He was still holding my hand and said we get a new shot at making a future, one different from the blood that runs through our veins. He said we can choose to be better than our past. I agreed then and asked him what future he chose. He said, 'you' then leaned in and kissed me. It was our first kiss."

Dad shakes his head. "Well, I guess better him than anyone else."

I laugh. "That day sealed our fate. We knew that was it for both of us."

Dad smiles and hands me the next envelope.

Sage,

That kiss took my breath away and until recently, stood in my mind as one of the best kisses of my life.

My mind raced. I knew I wanted to take you out on a date then but with limited options, I had to get creative.

I know it took me a few months to nail down the art of the perfect date.

I promise to make time even for small dates like this.

Head to the spot of our first date. Where I told you I was yours and you were mine.

Colt

The picnic dinner at the wagon wheel tracks at the back part of the property.

I get back in the truck. I can drive most of the way there, and I think of that night on the way.

He had packed the perfect picnic. Mom's friend chicken with fruit, chips, and brownies for dessert. It was my first picnic, and he picked the perfect spot. I love those wagon tracks, their history of the people walking them to a better life like we were doing.

I get as far as the creek when I park the truck and head out on foot. It's about a five-minute walk when I see Mom standing there.

She hugs me and smiles. "Colt had such a warm heart and to see him finally able to embrace that with you has been one of the greatest joys as a mother. I love you both so much."

She wastes no time and hands me the next envelope.

Sage,

From here, our journey heads into town. The more time I spent with you, the more time I wanted. We had to hide in front of the crowds, but we always seemed to find somewhere away from prying eyes to have a minute to ourselves during the day.

My favorite was when we would sneak away at lunchtime.

I promise to always sneak away and find time for us.

Colt

He must be talking about school, so I head into town to our old high school. We had so many great memories here. Even at school dances, he still found time to dance with me. It became second nature that we went to dances together as Blaze started dating.

As I pull into the school, I see Mac standing in front of the school.

I get out of the truck and give him a hug.

"This is where we met," he says to me.

"It is."

"I know I never said it, but that was one of the best days of my life. I didn't make friends easily, and you just barged your way right in and changed my life for the better. I don't think I ever thanked you for everything you did for me."

My eyes tear up. "I'd do it all over again without hesitation, Mac. You're family, always will be. Now stop, I've cried enough already today."

He laughs. "I hope you put on waterproof mascara. I think you have some more tears in the future today. Colt did good."

I shake my head as he hands me another envelope.

Sage,

I'm sure seeing Mac reminded you of how he joined our family. That time with you in the hospital, not knowing if you would ever wake up, was one of the scariest of my life. I begged and pleaded with God at first to make you okay. As time went on, I begged him that if he was going to take you, to take me too.

When you woke up, and those eyes looked into mine, I knew I'd marry you one day.

We got a bit bolder after that. Your next stop is the last date we had before you left town.

I promise to never hide you away again. I want everyone we pass to know you're mine, and I am yours.

In case you need another hint, it's also where we had our second date not too long ago.

Colt

"He really isn't leaving anything out, is he?"

"Nope, get going!" Mac says, pushing me toward my truck.

I head down to the café, trying to think who I might see next. As I walk in, I see Hunter sitting at what was always Colt and my booth. I smile and sit across from him.

"I think this means you're now part of the family," I joke with him. His face lights up.

"I can only hope," he says and looks into his coffee. I take a good look at him, and I know that look. It's how Colt and I looked when we were dancing around each other.

"Is she still keeping you at arm's length?" He looks up at me, surprised.

I can't help but roll my eyes. "Hunter, Megan is one who when focused, loses sight of everything else. It's a curse of all us Buchanan's. Right now, all she's seeing is the beauty shop. It's been her dream since we were kids. You need to push her to see past it. To see you."

He looks up at me. "She has me properly friend zoned."

I laugh. "The friend zone is safe. The more she reminds you of it, the bigger the chance she's reminding herself. Take a chance, Hunter. You'll only regret it if you don't."

He smiles. “It worked out well for you and Colt. I can only hope,” he says and hands me the next envelope.

I give his hand a squeeze. “Don’t give up on her.”

Sage,

The second chapter of us had a rocky start. I had been on the fence on what to do and then I saw you with Brice.

Everything was clear in a split instant. You were mine. I needed to stop pussyfooting around and make it happen.

That meant being true to my feelings. Regardless of how many times I wanted to punch Brice in the face, I’m thankful for him.

Because of him, I got the kick I needed to go after you. Because of him, we got our second chance. Because of him, we’re here now.

Because of him, I get to tell you every day I love you.

I promise to not only tell you but find a way to show you how much I love you every day.

Colt

I flip the card over, but there’s no hint of where to go next. I tap the card to my chin and think. Maybe I need to pay Brice a visit. I look over at Hunter, who’s watching me.

"You know, Hunter, it might be time for you to go on a date. Abby could use a night out."

Confusion covers his face. "Sage, I can't think of other women."

I laugh and hand him my card to read.

I watch understanding cross his face. "I'll talk to Abby. She'll play along. It's up to you."

I stand and pat his shoulder. "I'm off to hopefully find my man at the end of the trip down memory lane. This could be you soon. Just think about it."

I head to my truck and head across town to the clinic. I see Brice just inside.

"Right on time," he says.

"So, you're my next card?"

He holds up the envelope. "Yep. I will say I was a bit shocked when Colt came in here and thanked me for dating you. After the other night, I don't think I expected all this."

I laugh then get serious. "I never meant to hurt you or lead you on in any way. I was truly interested in dating. I thought I had to move on. I didn't think this was a possibility anymore."

"I get it. You're a great girl, but we just weren't a fit. No hard feelings, but it was great to date the girl I had a crush on in school."

I laugh. "We can stay friends, right?"

He hands me the envelope "As long as Colt won't kick my ass for it, I'd like that."

I shake my head.

"No promises." I laugh.

Sage,

Our first date this time around was everything I wish I could have given you the first time. Being able to dance with you was a memory I still play over and over in my head.

That kiss.

I'm still speechless when I think about it. It was perfect.

I promise to always take you out and show you off. To give you a reason to wear those dresses you love to buy. I promise to give you many reasons to keep filling our closet with those dresses.

Colt

The bar. This one is easy. I look back up at Brice.

"Thank you," I say, waving the card.

He smiles and nods his head.

I head back across town to the bar. It sounds like a pain but when I say across town, it's one stoplight and five blocks long. It takes five minutes at most, depending on how many people try to cross the street.

I park at the bar, and memories of this place are all over. From the night Colt and I came here not long ago to just the other night where Kelli thought she could get the best of us.

Even before then, we've all helped Jason with this place. I'm so proud of him. I head inside, and he looks up from taking inventory at the bar.

His contagious smile lights up his face. He walks around and picks me up in a bear hug and swings me around.

"I feel lucky I got a firsthand seat at watching all this unfold," he says and hands me my next envelope.

I look at Jason. He's the oldest, and I can't remember the last time I saw him even go out on a date. "You know your time is coming, right?"

He runs his hands through his hair.

"The right girl will accept this and want to help," he says, holding his arms out wide and talking about the bar. "She will have to be amazing to capture my attention."

I nod. "Just keep your heart open. You never know when she will walk into your life."

"Always the romantic," he says with a smile on his face.

"You don't by chance know how many more of these there are, do you?" I ask, holding up the envelope.

"Nope. Just doing as I was told." I smile.

Sage,

The night here in the bar was perfect. I love our dates, but I love having you to myself even more.

I love having dinner at home with you when you're relaxed and have your guard down.

I love watching TV on the couch with you.

I love falling asleep with you in my arms every night.

I love waking up with you in my arms every morning.

I love showering together, having breakfast together even before you get your coffee, and I love watching you cook in the kitchen.

I know your dream has always been to fill the house with love and laughter. I think we're off to a good start.

But I promise to fill the house with kids, family, and friends. I promise to make that house everything you've always dreamed of. Those dreams are mine too.

Colt

"Looks like I'm heading back to the ranch," I say.

He smiles. “Have fun. See you at dinner.”

With a quick hug, I’m back in my truck. Filling up the gas tank before heading back to the ranch, the thoughts of these last few weeks with Colt fill my head.

Even when I was in Memphis, he never felt that far away. Always doing something to show how much he loves me. Like today. Getting everyone we care about involved.

Once back home, I don’t see anyone outside, so I head into the house and find Abby at the dining room table.

“Colt get you in on this?” I ask, a bit confused.

“Yes, he did. I was so excited when he asked.”

I shake my head and take the envelope from her and sit at the table.

“You met Megan and Hunter, right?”

“Yeah, they’re such a cute couple.”

“That’s the problem. My sister refuses to see what is right in front of her. Like she expects him to always be there. I suggested to Hunter that maybe he needs to start dating again. It worked on Colt when I started dating Brice.”

“It would open her eyes for sure.”

“Maybe you could make some off-handed comment about how cute Hunter is, ask if he’s seeing anyone, make it look like you’re interested. I suggested Hunter talk to you about a few dates. You need to see the town, and Megan needs an eye-opener. It's a win-win."

She chews on the inside of her cheek. "I don't want to make her mad, but I'm always up for a little matchmaking."

I laugh and open my envelope.

Sage,

Abby is new to the ranch, but she's such a big part of our story. More than I ever realized.

I hated being away from you while you were in Memphis but looking back, the time allowed me to think about us, about you, about me.

I was able to make plans we were always talking about.

I know you love to travel, and I wanted to be by your side every day you were in Memphis but with the short notice, I couldn't do it.

My promise to you is to help you finish your bucket list. Mom and Dad always took us to the lake house. I promise to follow in their footsteps and take us someplace once a year. A vacation for us, for our family.

I want that family we dreamed of, and I only want it with you.

I love how passionate you are with the horses you train and work with. So many times, I will come around the barn just to watch you. You're so involved with what you're doing, you never see me. That's okay. I like being able to just watch.

Colt

I don't realize tears are running down my face until Abby speaks up.

"Oh no, he made you cry! Is it a good thing or a bad thing?"

I smile. "All good things today. I guess this means you're an official member of the ranch."

Her smile lights up her face.

I get up and head out to the horse pens and find Riley. When she sees me, her whole face lights up. It seems to be the trend today.

"You have an envelope for me?"

"I have two things for you! Envelope first. And I have to say what he's doing is so romantic!"

"Colt has his moments when he wants to make sure I know how he feels, good or bad."

We both laugh then I read the note.

Sage,

I can't tell you how many times over the last several years I've stood and watched you working here. It's calming to me even on our worst days.

You're an amazing woman as shown by how easily you can gain the most untrusting horse's trust.

Seeing how you've taken Riley under your wing and helped her blossom has been amazing to watch.

Turn around, take in all you've built. We all busted our asses for this right here, but it's because of you, we're here. Your dream was so infectious, we had to be part of it.

I love working this land as much as you do, and I hope to grow old and be buried on this ranch with you.

There's one more stop on our journey today. It's our spot. The spot I could run away to when things got too hard. The spot where you're always there even when you aren't. The spot we had our biggest first, the last time we were together, and this time.

Our spot. See you there, my love.

Colt

Once again, this man has me in tears and as I look up, I see Riley dangling a key to one of the four-wheelers.

"I was told you would need this," she says.

I take the key and hug her. Then I head out to our cabin, to find Colt.

Chapter 24

Colt

My phone pings.

Riley: She just left. Good luck!

I've been getting texts all day, letting me know Sage made it to the next location and when she left, so I can make sure I'm here and ready.

I don't think I've ever been this nervous a day in my life. Today is a huge turning point for Sage and me. One I hope will be the start of the life we've planned together.

I have about fifteen minutes before she gets here, so I make sure everything is ready. I check on the food in the kitchen. Mom's famous crockpot lasagna and garlic bread with her famous chocolate brownies and ice cream for dessert.

The table is set with candles. I've covered the main living area with candles and have a fire going in the fireplace. As night falls, it will get a bit chilly. There are flower petals and more candles covering the bedroom, and everything she would need for a relaxing bath.

I turn on some quiet, slow music from my playlist and go over the words in my head. I hear the rumble of the four-wheeler's engine and know it's showtime.

I take a deep breath, grab the last envelope, and stand in the middle of the small living room, facing the front door, waiting.

I see the handle turn and the door open. There she is in the sexiest shorts I've ever seen. She looks around and surprise registers on her face.

"Colt, what's going on?" she asks, still taking everything in.

"You have one more envelope," I say with a smile and hand her the envelope in my hands. I watch her read it.

Sage,

All day I've taken you to some of the spots that hold my favorite memories of us, with the people who mean the most to us.

Now it's time to make a new memory. Followed by many more.

I want the life we planned—kids, vacations, late nights, early mornings, family, and friends with you.

I want to watch you teach our kids to ride a horse. I want to teach them to love this land like we do. I want to sit on our front porch and watch our grandkids play and hold your hand.

I want to spoil you, show you what you mean to me daily.

You carry my heart with you daily, you own my soul, and you're my reason for living. Life isn't complete without you.

Now I have a very important question for you. When you're ready....

Colt

As I see her eyes water, I get down on one knee and wait for her eyes to find me again. When they do, I almost forget everything I had planned.

There's so much awe and love on her face, it makes my heart race.

"I love you more today than yesterday, and I will love you more tomorrow than I do today. Be my wife and let me show you that you're my everything. Marry me?"

"Yes!" she says and falls into my arms, wrapping her arms around my neck. My lips find hers for a moment before I pull back with the need to get the ring on her finger.

When she sees it, she gasps, "Colt?"

"I want to take credit for the ring, but you have to thank Mom and Dad for that one," I say, and she cries while looking at the ring. I know what it means to her, so I just hold her and let the emotions run through her.

After a few minutes, I ask, "You hungry?"

"Yes, I haven't eaten since breakfast."

I shake my head. "Should have made you eat at the café."

I pick her up, carry her to the table, and sit her in the chair I set for her. I pull the bread out of the oven and bring the crockpot over to the table.

I serve her first before filling my plate and sitting across from her. Seeing the ring on her hand, I reach across the table and take her hand, running my thumb over it. Something about the ring being there calms and soothes me. It's also a major turn on. My cock has been hard ever since I slid it onto her finger.

"What kind of wedding do you want?" I ask her.

"I always thought I'd be married at the ranch church. I know what I want my dress to look like. Besides that, I don't know. I guess I always pictured you guys standing with me. Now I have to fight over who is on my side or yours."

"Well, what about doing couples instead and have them scattered all over the front of the church. No sides. There won't be any sides for the guests either."

"I love it. What about the reception at the event barn?"

"It's perfect. How long do you need to plan? Because next weekend would be great." I watch her eyes go big.

"Colt!"

I smile "The sooner the better. Just let me know when so I can plan our honeymoon. I want to surprise you."

"I can't wait to travel with you. Almost more so than our wedding." She laughs.

We make some plans over dinner then I bring out dessert and pull her onto my lap as I feed her every bite.

I love watching her enjoy a meal I prepared for her. Knowing I provided for her makes my chest swell.

After she has finished eating, I carry her into the bedroom for my dessert.

Chapter 25

Sage

The next morning, we head back to the main house. When we walk in, Colt yells, "She said yes!"

Everyone yells and cheers. After breakfast, I ask Megan, Riley, and Abby to stay behind for a bit.

Once the guys are gone, I say, "I need your help."

"Planning a wedding? Of course!" Abby is excited.

"That too but first, I need to issue a little revenge."

"Uh oh. Kelli?" Megan asks.

"Yep," I say, popping the 'p.'

There's a reason I've asked Megan to stay. I am so glad she's on my side. She's crazy!

So, after a few phone calls, Jason promises to let us know the next time Kelli is at the bar, so we can put our plan into motion.

• • • • • • • • • • •

It only takes four days before Kelli shows up at the bar. I get the text from Megan. She's on her way there to make sure she doesn't leave while I convince Colt to go down with me. Being it's Friday night, I have a plan.

I find him just getting out of the shower, and I can't help but let my eyes trail down his still-wet, hard abs. My eyes follow a drop of water that slides from his hard nipple and follows the creases of his abs before running all the way down to his cock. What I wouldn't give to be that drop of water right now.

"Sage," he growls in a warning. It snaps me out of my thoughts and back to the task at hand.

"I was thinking maybe we could go to the bar tonight. There's a live band playing I want to check out. Plus, I wouldn't mind dancing with you again," I say and lick my lips.

"Of course, love. I promised to always give you a reason to wear those dresses. Go pick one out."

We get dressed and once on our way, I text Megan. She says Kelli just ordered drink number two. Funny how no guys are willing to buy her drinks anymore.

We walk in hand in hand, and I can tell when Colt sees her. His whole body goes rigid.

"I got this, Colt. Don't you worry." That's when he sees Megan.

"What did you do?" he asks.

"Me?" I smirk. "Nothing yet."

I pull Colt to the bar and make sure my left side faces Kelli as I sit with a stool between us.

Jason walks up and hands us both a beer. Then he says a little louder than normal, "Hey lovebirds, how's the wedding plans going?"

Out of the corner of my eye, I see Kelli's head snap my way. I use my left hand with the ring on my finger to push some hair out of my face.

"Perfect. We're letting Blaze and Riley have their day before we jump headfirst into plans."

Jason walks off to grab drinks for a few people at the other end of the bar.

Colt leans in and whispers in my ear, "I know what you're doing."

I smile. "I'm not done yet."

"Have your fun but make it quick. I want to get you on the dance floor, so I can get my hands on your sexy body."

His low gruff timbre sets my body on fire and causes my nipples to stiffen at how turned on I am.

I smile and bite my lip while checking Colt out.

He growls and uses his thumb to pull my lips from between my teeth before leaning in and kissing it quick.

This time, I turn to Kelli and fake a concerned look.

"You look tired."

"Just waking up early," she says.

I smile and grab Colt's hand to head out to dance.

"Yeah, those morning wakeup calls can be a real bitch." I see rage cross her face before I continue, "If you don't slink away now, this is just the beginning of the fun I have planned. Remember my brother owns this bar..."

I smile and look at Jason who winks at her. She storms off as Colt pulls me to the dance floor.

"What was that all about?"

"That's a good reason to always stay on Megan's good side. Megan set up a morning four a.m. wakeup call for her every morning."

Colt shakes his head and smiles.

"Oh, it gets worse. When she answers it, she plays a loud air horn in her ear. If she doesn't answer, it calls every five minutes until she does. Oh, and every morning, it calls from a new number, so she can't block it."

Colt throws his head back and laughs. Then his eyes meet mine. He brings his hand to the side of my face.

"Remind me to not get on your bad side," he says and runs this thumb over my mouth. "Have I told you how sexy you look tonight?"

"I don't think that's something you can say too much."

He smiles. "Well, you look sexy, Sage. This dress looks amazing on you. So much so, I don't think I can let you leave my side tonight. The moment I do, every guy in here will pounce."

"Guess it's a good thing the only guy I want is you."

"Damn right, love."

I smile. We spend the night dancing to the live music and enjoying time together.

The life I've dreamed of is just ahead of us, and I couldn't be happier.

Epilogue

Sage

Three Months Later

I'm in my room watching Riley slip into her wedding dress and am an equal mix of excited and sad. Today, Riley becomes my sister for real. I'm so excited. I love this girl, and she has been so good for Blaze.

I'm sad because Blaze is the first one of us to get married. I know I'm not far behind him, but he's the first, and it will change the whole family dynamic. I know it's for the better, but I can't help but mourn the loss of just the six of us.

My phone buzzes, pulling me from my thoughts.

Colt: My room. Now.

The girls took over our room for the bride to get ready since it's the biggest and best equipped. I can't help but think we started a tradition here today. That means Colt has been forced from our room. The guys are getting ready in a room at the other end of the hall, so Colt must have snuck away.

"Hey, I'll be right back," I call to Riley who's in the bathroom with Megan doing her hair.

Then I slip out the door and into Colt's old room right next door. Colt has me pressed up against the door as soon as it's closed. His eyes rake down my body.

He lets out a low groan in seeing me in my maid of honor dress. "You look so damn beautiful, Sage. How am I supposed to keep my hands off you today?"

I shrug. "You're not." I smile as he rests his forehead on mine. "You know, I always had a fantasy of sleeping with the best man at a wedding," I whisper.

I see Colt smile. "Guess I'm your fantasy come true tonight, love."

I laugh. He's right. When Riley asked me to be her maid of honor, I was torn about it. We had always planned that I'd stand with Blaze. From the time we were kids, we knew we'd be each other's 'best man,' so I talked with him.

He was over the moon that Riley asked me to be her maid of honor and that she trusts me like he does. Riley fits into our lives. She asked Megan and Abby to be bridesmaids, along with Lilly, the truck driver who brought her to Rock Springs. So, we have Lilly to thank for bringing Riley into our lives.

Blaze then asked Colt to be his best man. I joked that it's because Colt wouldn't put up with anyone else touching me, but I know how close the two are. He also asked Mac, Jason, and Hunter to be his groomsmen. I had to insist that Hunter and Megan be paired up. He needs all the help he can get.

"Two more months," Colt says, pulling me from my thoughts. "Two more months, then it's our turn," he says into my neck and kisses where my neck and shoulder meet.

I wrap my arms around his neck. "I can't wait until it's our turn."

"Longest two months of my life," he growls, making me laugh again.

When there's a knock on the door, we both jump.

"If you two are almost done, it's time to head down for pictures," Megan singsongs, causing us both to smile.

The family has gotten used to us always sneaking away for our moments alone. Blaze and Riley have them too, so I'm sure Blaze is a caged bear today, being he hasn't seen Riley.

Colt gives my ass a good squeeze and kisses my neck again. "Soon as you're done walking down the aisle, I'm messing up your makeup."

My thighs squeeze together. "Can't wait," I moan. "Take Blaze to the back of the barn and text me when he's there."

Colt nods and heads out to get Blaze. They're getting married in the barn here on this side of the property, and we're doing a few photos of Blaze standing at the back of the barn at one corner and reaching around the corner to hold Riley's hand. He won't be able to see her, but the camera will get them both.

Riley is really excited about this picture idea, and I think the red clapboard siding of the barn will be the perfect background for it.

I head back to my room to find Riley and make our way to the barn.

• • • • • • • • • • • •

Riley is officially stuck with us. My big strong Blaze, who I've only ever seen cry twice in my life, does so watching Riley walk down the aisle to him. Colt and I lock eyes during the ceremony, and I can't tell you what happened; I never took my eyes off Colt.

He makes good on his promise too. The second everyone is done with pictures and heading to the event barn, he pulls me into the barn office and properly messes up my makeup. Then he helps me fix it again before heading out to the reception.

He hasn't left my side, and I've loved dancing with him. We're now giving my poor feet a break, and he has me pulled into his lap at our table. I look around and see Megan and Hunter dancing. Mom and Dad are on the dance floor too. Blaze and Riley are at their table. Honestly, I'm surprised they haven't snuck out to their honeymoon yet.

They're heading down to the lake house a few hours from here. After a week, they've invited us all down to give Riley the full lake house family experience. That means the whole family. They also just announced Riley is pregnant and you can still feel the buzz in the air.

Sadly, Megan is staying home this year. Part of me hopes it's to spend some time with Hunter.

"So, what do you think, my love?" Colt asks.

"About what?"

He chuckles. “All this. Is this how you picture our reception?”

I smile. “For the most part, just different people. I have a bunch of people I met while traveling who are excited to meet you, see the ranch, and be part of our day.”

He nuzzles my neck. “I can’t wait to meet them.”

“So, you going to tell me about this big awesome honeymoon you have planned?”

He smiles. “Nope. It’s my surprise to you, I will say I can’t wait to travel with you.”

I smile and rest my head on his shoulder. “I can’t wait either.”

Want 2 more bonus Sage and Colt Epilogues? Get them + 2 free bonus stories when you sign up for my newsletter!

Sign up for my newsletter here.

https://www.kacirose.com/SCbe

The Rock Springs Texas series continues with Hunter and Megan's story.

The Cowboy and His Obsession

More Books by Kaci M. Rose

Rock Springs Texas Series

The Cowboy and His Runaway – Blaze and Riley

The Cowboy and His Best Friend – Sage and Colt

The Cowboy and His Obsession – Megan and Hunter

The Cowboy and His Sweetheart – Jason and Ella

The Cowboy and His Secret – Mac and Sarah

Rock Springs Weddings Novella

Rock Springs Box Set 1-5 + Bonus Content

Cowboys of Rock Springs

The Cowboy and His Mistletoe Kiss – Lilly and Mike

The Cowboy and His Valentine – Maggie and Nick

The Cowboy and His Vegas Wedding – Royce and Anna
The Cowboy and His Angel – Abby and Greg
The Cowboy and His Christmas Rockstar – Savannah and Ford
The Cowboy and His Billionaire – Brice and Kayla

Connect with Kaci M. Rose

Kaci M. Rose writes steamy small town cowboys. She also writes under Kaci Rose and there she writes wounded military heroes, giant mountain men, sexy rock stars, and even more there. Connect with her below!

Website
Facebook
Kaci Rose Reader's Facebook Group
Goodreads
Book Bub
Join Kaci M. Rose's VIP List (Newsletter)

About Kaci M Rose

Kaci M Rose writes cowboy, hot and steamy cowboys set in all town anywhere you can find a cowboy.

She enjoys horseback riding and attending a rodeo where is always looking for inspiration.

Kaci grew on a small farm/ranch in Florida where they raised cattle and an orange grove. She learned to ride a four-wheeler instead of a bike (and to this day still can't ride a bike) and was driving a tractor before she could drive a car.

Kaci prefers the country to the city to this day and is working to buy her own slice of land in the next year or two!

Kaci M Rose is the Cowboy Romance alter ego of Author Kaci Rose.

See all of Kaci Rose's Books here.

Please Leave a Review!

I love to hear from my readers! Please **head over to your favorite store and leave a review** of what you thought of this book!

Made in the USA
Columbia, SC
30 January 2024

30724387R00143